THERE ARE
NO COINCIDENCES

THERE ARE
NO COINCIDENCES

"AN ORIENT SUCCESS"

ANOTHER SPY THRILLER BY

PETER MARSHALL

Paperback: 978-1-63767-651-6
eBook: 978-1-63767-652-3
Library of Congress Control Number: 2021924114

This is a work of fiction.

Ordering Information:

BookTrail Agency
8838 Sleepy Hollow Rd.
Kansas City, MO 64114

CONTENTS

FOREWORD

So what REALLY happened to Marina Peters? This is the third part of her astonishing story.

It all began when her handsome on-line computer date turned out to be a spy – he was *"The Russian Lieutenant"* – and after their romantic first meeting was disturbed by MI5, his murderous accomplices poisoned her with deadly Ricin. But her funeral was faked by the British and American secret services, and she recovered to become "Samantha Lord", a new CIA agent. In *"After the Funeral"*, she began a new career, working in the dangerous world of international espionage. Among other missions, this eventually took her to a new assignment in Japan – where Nikolai Aldanov, her Russian "date", had been sent to a dead-end job as 'punishment' for his failures as a GUR agent.

This was part of a plan – there are no coincidences in the ruthless world of the secret agencies in their pursuit of national security. The dramatic reunion of "Samantha" with the Russian produced the right result for the CIA and for Marina's experienced British mentor, the quietly creative Tom Spencer.

To follow this successful Oriental mission, Tom had a rather different plan in mind – and yet another new identity for the future of his protégé.

Again, I am indebted to a couple of friends with more detailed knowledge than I have of the murky world of the secret services – they know who they are, and I want to thank them for their good advice. All the activities and the individuals who are part of my story are fictitious and any resemblance to real people, alive or dead, is entirely coincidental. Also, although many of the locations described in the book are based on my own travel experiences and research, all the events described are also completely creative fiction.

Enjoy the story.
Peter Marshall

CHAPTER 1

GUNMEN IN THE BAR

It was a warm October evening and the Friday shoppers were swarming through the Ginza, Tokyo's most fashionable centre. To visitors from overseas, the combination of elegant stores and boutique shops, large and small, together with the brilliant lighting displays and advertising signs, seemed like a combination of London's Regent Street and New York's Times Square – plus some of the Las Vegas extravagance. As the window shoppers crowded the sidewalks, hustling past those carrying their purchases in bags displaying the names of the leading stores, it became harder and harder to move without stepping into the roadway and creating problems for the frustrated taxi drivers.

Moving slowly through the heaving throng were two men enjoying the spectacle. One of them was Nikolai Aldanov who could not take his eyes from the pretty young Japanese girls, mostly walking and chattering in groups or pairs. "There are thousands of them, Endo-san – where do they all come from?" he asked his colleague and new friend from the Russian embassy, Hideki Endo.

It was the end of Nikolai's first week in his new job as the defence department attache at the embassy in the Akasaka district of Tokyo. With him that evening was his locally-engaged assistant and interpreter Hideki and after an intensive few days of briefings and the handover from his predecessor, Nikolai had been ready to accept the offer of "a night on the town".

He had flown into Tokyo's Narita airport on a direct flight from Moscow on the previous Monday afternoon and he was relieved to spot the only welcome sign he could understand. It was being held high above the heads of the waiting crowd in the arrivals area of the terminal building – *"Aldanov dobro pozhalovat"*. He had to push his way through the jostling mass to reach the man holding the sign in Russian who introduced himself as Dimitri from the embassy and showed his security pass by way of proof. He welcomed Nikolai warmly and as they walked to the baggage retrieval area, he explained that he was the current defence attache at the Russian embassy and that he was preparing to leave.

"I am so pleased you are here safely," he said, "because I am already packed and ready to return home to my family in Moscow on Wednesday".

Like Nikolai, Dimitri was a tall and strongly-built man, in sharp contrast to most of the smaller and trim Japanese people surrounding them. After another wait at the luggage carousel, he led the way with their baggage trolley, through the swirling crowds to the entrance for the Narita Express train to the city. He said this trip would take about 50 minutes compared with two hours or more to drive by car because of the traffic congestion. Nikolai was quickly recognising from his first experiences, both at the airport and then on the train, that Tokyo was simply teeming with people and activity, and yet everything somehow seemed efficiently and impressively organised. He was also relieved to spot that most of the important information signs seemed to be translated into English, which he could understand.

The train journey was fast and comfortable, although the passengers and their luggage were tightly packed. On the way to the city, Dimitri explained that he would be taking Nikolai to a hotel close to the embassy where he would stay for the next two or three days. Then from Wednesday, he would be able to move into the apartment which he would be vacating and which he described as both comfortable and convenient for a single man. This was one piece of reassuring news for Nikolai who was feeling very apprehensive about both his new job and the unfamiliar environment. His briefings before he left Moscow had focused on his new duties, the organization at the Japanese embassy, his documentation and travel plans and his personal financial arrangements. "You will discover the rest when you get there," he was told.

From Tokyo's central station, the two diplomats took a taxi from the orderly rank of shiny black vehicles and Nikolai was immediately impressed by the smartly dressed and polite driver as well as by the immaculate interior of the car with its white, lacy antimacassars and seat covers. What a contrast, he thought, with the untidy and often old and damaged taxis used by Moscow's sullen cab drivers.

Because of the time change, he was feeling tired and could only listen quietly as Dimitri provided some commentary about Tokyo's traffic, the city road system and some of the prominent buildings until they reached the Mimaru Hotel in the Akasaka district. At the check-in counter, the smiling receptionist handled the paperwork quickly and took Nikolai's passport before a polite and smartly uniformed porter bowed and collected his luggage. As he prepared to leave, Dimitri said he hoped Nikolai would sleep well and added that he would be there in the lobby to collect him at 8.30 the next morning.

The travel-weary and jet-lagged new arrival followed the porter to the lift and up to his assigned room. It was on the third floor with a view across the city where a main feature was the prominent, red-coloured radio tower. The room was rather small, he thought, but it was attractively furnished with colourful pictures of Japan on the walls and with a TV showing Japanese news. After retrieving his essential toiletries from his carry-on bag, he used the phone to order a beer and a club sandwich, which he found listed in English in the room service menu. He was still setting his morning alarm call on the modern, digital communications bedside unit when there was a knock on the door and a polite young waiter delivered his bedtime tray – and bowed before leaving. Before long, Nikolai was impressed by the service and soon he was trying to sleep, but with so many new experiences still flashing in his mind.

He was jarred awake by his alarm at 7am, struggled for a moment to remember where he was, and then began to prepare for his first day in Japan. His two suitcases were still unpacked, but he managed to find the right clothes for the day ahead and after a wake-up shower, he realised he was quite hungry and decided to find the hotel restaurant for breakfast. The hotel was regularly used by foreign businessmen and tourists and a charming Japanese waitress bowed with a welcoming smile as she showed him the multi-lingual menu. It was in four languages, but not in Russian he noted. Nikolai's English was good enough to recognise some of the items, but instead he ordered coffee and chose to go to the buffet and make his own selections of familiar breakfast cereals, fruit, and croissants. He did not delay and he was back in the reception area a few minutes before 8.30 ready to go with his briefcase. Dimitri was already there, with a chauffeured embassy car waiting outside.

The short drive took them to the Russian Embassy building which was in a row of smart, multi-storey modern office blocks. At first sight, it looked rather smaller than Nikolai was expecting. But there was the familiar Russian flag fluttering above the front entrance doors which led into a modern tower block. They went through a metal detector into the lobby area, watched carefully by a security guard, and then took a flight of stairs up to the first-floor office area and a room which Dimitri described as "your new home from tomorrow". It was bright and modern, with a view of the attractive garden and lawns at the back of the building, and there were two desks – the larger one was for the attache, explained Dimitri, and the second one was for his Japanese assistant Endo who would be arriving at 9-o-clock.

"Is it usual to have local people working in this sort of job here?" asked a rather surprised Nikolai. He was reassured by the response that there were about twelve locally-engaged staff at the Embassy in various support roles and he added that Endo was an experienced administrator who previously worked in a Japanese government department. Then noting the concern in the question, he added: "He does have security clearance and even more important, lots of local knowledge."

They sat at a small conference table and Dimitri began to outline their plans for the day – "This is our one-day handover," he said, adding quickly that it was not a very demanding job so it would not take long. He began by telling Nikolai that the Ambassador was General Igor Malinov, a former KGB officer, who had been in the post for nearly three years. This meant that he had a wide range of political and diplomatic contacts, both in Tokyo and in Moscow as well as around the country and he added quietly: "That means that whoever you meet during your time here, he will probably hear about it on his grapevine before you get back to the office, so take care. And by the way, you have an appointment with the Ambassador to welcome you at 11 o clock".

Dimitri went on to describe his day-to-day routines and responsibilities until promptly at nine, his Japanese assistant Hideki Endo arrived and was introduced. "Endo-san knows everything," said Dimitri, as his assistant bowed and welcomed the new attache with a polite "*dobroye utro*", to demonstrate that he had learned some useful Russian phrases.

"You can be confident that Endo-san will always know exactly where you should go and when, and what you should take with you," continued Dimitri. "He knows where all the information and background files are kept. He will make your appointments and fix any travel arrangements you need."

Then Dimitri added: "And Endo-san will also be very happy to show you around all the best places in Tokyo as he did when I arrived here last year." At this, the two of them shared a knowing look and laughed.

Nikolai could only imagine what they had in mind, but he liked his first impressions of Endo, who was a short, stocky man in his mid-30's, with a warm smile and a confident style. He went back to his own desk to unlock the filing cabinets and a few minutes later, he brought back a stack of blue files which he placed carefully between the two diplomats. Dimitri then worked his way through a series of documents with Nikolai and highlighted the subjects requiring action and explained that these were mostly related to ongoing tasks, all of which had been assigned to him by the Ambassador. Some files related to forthcoming visits to Japan by government ministers and other military VIPs from Moscow as well as requests for information from the defence ministry.

He then took out four files from his own locked desk drawer and explained that these were the personal records of the Russian military officers who were currently serving in diplomat roles in Japan. Pointing to a map of the country on the office wall, he said they were based in the consular offices in the cities of Saporro and Hakomate in the more distant northern island of Hokkaido and at Osaka and Niigata in the main island of Honchu. "These guys are your defence department team," he added. "So you will need to keep in regular contact with them and also work with them when you are travelling around the country to follow up on some of the sensitive political issues in those areas. I am sure the Ambassador will outline some of these at your meeting with him and I can fill in any gaps for you afterwards".

While they were reviewing and discussing the files, Hideki Endo brought them expresso coffees and later reminded them when it was time to go upstairs to see "the boss".

General Malinov was seated behind his large oak desk when they arrived at the ambassador's spacious modern-style office and Nikolai was surprised to find him wearing military uniform, complete with an extensive array of medal ribbons. He gruffly welcomed the new arrival, waving him to sit in a facing chair close to the desk as Dimitri went to sit at the back of the room.

"I know all about your history, Aldanov," he began, without a word of welcome. "It seems that you made a bit of a mess of things when you were in GRU, but you are not the only one to do that and I am told you have been doing a decent job at the Ministry since then. They probably told you in Moscow that this is one of the quieter overseas assignments, but there are a few rumblings which we are here to keep a close eye on. You may hear about things which you should report to me, but remember that I have a quite separate specialised unit here with three experienced GRU agents. So you can forget that you once had a spell as an agent, so do not get involved in any intelligence matters. Do you understand?"

"Yes, of course, sir," said Aldanov, trying to appear confident.

"Right," said the General, banging his fist on his desk for greater effect as he continued: "Well, the first thing to understand as my defence department attache is that America has a huge influence over the military scene here in Japan. They have about twenty army, air force and navy bases spread around the country, most of them down south on the island of Okinawa. Altogether, there are more than 40,000 service personnel here, plus their families in many cases, so you can run into Americans almost anywhere and that does not include the tourists. This may surprise you, but Kozlov will explain to you that diplomats from all the embassies here in Tokyo are able to use the facilities of the American Club as associate members. It is a great place for meeting people but if you go there, the golden rule is to listen to everything but don't say too much".

He paused and buzzed for his assistant to bring a jug of iced water and to serve them in three glasses before continuing.

"Now to the serious matters," he said. "I need to explain that the biggest long-term issue here is about the Kuril Islands at the North of Japan, which is quite close to the Russian coast. We took possession of these islands during the war and since 1945 every Japanese leader has tried to negotiate their return to Japan. They still call them the Northern Territories and our position has always been that we will not even discuss the matter unless they undertake to never allow the USA to base their military there. And so the argument goes on, year after year, with various rumblings beneath the surface, so I am sure we will be talking more about this during your time here. Any questions?"

"No, sir," replied Aldanov. "I understand that this is an important matter because it was also highlighted to me in Moscow. I will keep it in mind as I find my way around and I look forward to any future assignments from you, of course. I obviously have a great deal to learn, but I am ready."

The General turned to Dimitri and thanked him for his work in the past year and wished him well in his next assignment – and then indicated that the meeting was over.

"Well, that was short and sweet," said Nikolai as they returned to the office. "So, what happens next?"

"With him, it's difficult to say but don't worry. He is very well organised and when he wants something, it is always very clear and you will find that Endo-san understands everything better than anyone else," said Dimitri looking appreciatively towards his Japanese assistant. "So let me walk you round the building to meet everyone else."

He then took Nikolai to the adjoining offices to meet his new colleagues, all anxious to meet the newcomer from Moscow. They started with the business and economic attache and then the political attache, who both welcomed him with warm words and offers of any help he may need. Next came a brief visit to the busy consular and visa section on the ground floor and an introduction to the counsellor in charge. This was followed by a long conversation with the information officer, who appeared to be the only woman in the senior team.

Then they moved upstairs again to the large open office next to the Ambassador's room to meet the head of the intelligence section, who Dimitri introduced as Pavel Levitsky – which was a name which Nikolai recognised from his time on the GRU staff in Moscow.

The recognition was mutual as Levitsky said sternly by way of welcome: "Aha! So the Russian Lieutenant is here. We saw that you were all over the front pages in the Western press a few months ago – woman trouble I remember. Not a good thing for one of our agents. Actually, you are lucky to be here and not in a Siberian camp".

Nikolai just nodded, looking contrite and deciding not to respond beyond a quiet "Yes, I know". Looking around, he took an interest in the four work units in the area, all equipped with computers and complex electronic equipment, only two of which appeared to be occupied at the time. Pavel called out: "Hey, Mikhail and Ilia – say hello to our new naval man from Moscow. This is Nikolai and he takes over from Dimitri this week". They gave a friendly wave from their desks and he added that the other agent Ivan was away on a mission".

As they walked away, Livitsky gave the new man a knowing grin and said, "I guess some of this looks familiar to you, but you have moved on since those days. You will appreciate that my team here works in our own secret world, quite separate from everything else going on in the embassy. You may even know the names of my three agents, but if so you will also know that you keep our names to yourself. Okay?"

Nikolai assured the spy chief that he fully understood the situation and Livitsky wished him well in his new job, adding pointedly but with a warmer smile: "Enjoy Tokyo, but not too much. Some of the women can be dangerous."

"Now you know," said Dimitri when they returned to his office, "It is a pretty small team here, but we all get on well and support each other as you will find at the weekly Monday morning briefings with the General. And you will not need to see much of Levitsky. They keep themselves to themselves. So I suggest you just read yourself in with these active files over the next couple of days and remember that Endo-san will always be able to help. And if he doesn't have all the answers, he can tell you who to ask. Then there is Olga who runs the admin here and she will give you your membership card for the American Club."

And with that, Dimitri began to collect his personal belongings including the photographs on his desk, and pack them into his brief case and a cardboard box. He then wished Nikolai well, shook hands and with a final "good luck" he went to back to his flat to prepare for the journey home to Moscow the next day. Nikolai sat at his new desk, deep in thought, and was relieved when Endo said: "Okay, sir. Let me start by introducing you to the office systems here, starting with the computer programmes…"

The rest of the week was mainly occupied with studying the files left by his predecessor and getting helpful background information from his assistant. The largest set of files, as he had expected from his meeting with the Ambassador, was simply titled "KURILS". This was a name he had never heard before his briefing in Moscow, but as he read through the documents, he discovered more details about this dispute between Japan and Russia which dated back to 1945. He found a long and detailed narrative, including records of the annual but unproductive negotiations which had taken place between the two governments, sometimes even at the level of Presidents. And he was surprised to discover that in various parts of Japan, there were still private protest organizations whose objective was to encourage the relevant local and national government departments to push for the return of the islands. The documents also named some of the leaders of the movement including one man, whose family was among the thousands evicted from the islands by the Russians. He was the leader of the League of Chishima Habomai Islands Residents – with a footnote which explained that Chishima was the historic Japanese name for the Kuril Islands, but which were still also known in Japan as the Northern Territories.

Nikolai absorbed this information and then turned to his assistant to ask rather cautiously: "Endo-san, about this Kurils subject, it looks like a big problem here. Is this protest league very active? How does it affect us?"

"No, no, no sir," replied Endo, dismissively. "Do not worry. It is not important. All we have to do is prepare the documents for the meetings between the various Russian and Japanese ministers whenever they take place, usually once a year. I will let you know if there is anything new."

Nikolai recognized that it was not a subject which his assistant wanted to discuss further, but otherwise there seemed to be nothing urgent or contentious in the files.

During this first week of studying files and settling in, he was pleased to see more of the other embassy officers who dropped into the office from time to time to offer any help, to share a coffee break and also take him to nearby sushi bars for lunch and an introduction to Japanese menus. They shared their experiences and gave their advice on living in Japan – but made no mention of his previous appointment as a GRU agent, which made him believe that maybe the episode was not widely known. One day, he found Mikhail and Ilia having lunch and they invited him to join them. He took great care not to mention the work of the GRU as they chatted, but encouragingly he was able to strike a friendly chord with Ilia, the younger of the pair, who was also new to Tokyo.

On the Wednesday morning, Olga, the attractive and friendly administrator from the Ambassador's office, told him that the apartment vacated by Dimitri was now ready for him. So, at the end of the day, he checked out of the hotel and was taken by her to the two-room apartment. He was pleased to discover it was within easy walking distance from the embassy. It was in a modern block, among several apartments owned by the Russian government for Embassy staff, and as Olga showed him around and explained the various facilities, he was pleased to discover that it was comfortably furnished and well-equipped. He soon settled in and enjoyed a quiet and relaxed evening, adjusting to the time change and learning his way around the local TV channels.

When Friday afternoon arrived, he decided it was time to ask Endo: "How about that tour of the town which Dimitri mentioned – is this evening good for you?" "Sure thing," replied Endo enthusiastically and they set off at about 7pm by taxi to the busy Ginza district. "It is the best place to start," he said.

Nikolai was amazed, not only by all the pretty girls among the mass of slowly moving people, but also by the lavish window displays in large department stores, the illuminations and bold advertising signs, the noise of music and the hooting of the traffic. After struggling their way through the crowd for nearly an hour, he was relieved when Endo suggested a drink. He led Nikolai along a side road and past several small cafes until they reached what he described as "my favourite bar". It was busy and they inched their way through the mostly Japanese customers, plus just a few obvious tourists, towards the bar. Some of the drinkers were entertaining their friends in the crowd loudly and off-key with karaoke songs. The words were on a wide screen above the bar and Nikolai noted that they were in both Japanese characters and English and one local man was singing a familiar song, his face and neck flushed red with the effects of alcohol experienced by so many Japanese. The crowd of would-be Sinatras were joining in and Nikolai was enjoying his first taste of sake…

"…I travelled each and every highway, but more, much more than this, I did it my way…

…when suddenly, the hubbub of the evening was broken by the sound of gunfire and screams behind them.

Nikolai and Endo both fell to the floor together with others around them. The Russian clasped his shoulder and shouted out "I've been shot" as he turned to his colleague – but he was alarmed to see that Endo appeared to be unconscious beside him. In the panic which followed, it was hard to tell who had been shot and who had been trampled in the crush to escape from the only door. Within a few minutes, police sirens screeched in the road outside and uniformed officers found that in the mayhem, some of the customers had bravely tried to wrestle with two suspected gunmen and had seized their weapons. There were more sirens as ambulances arrived through the traffic and the fleeing crowds. It took several more minutes to bring some semblance of order and relative calm inside the bar.

The emergency teams found more than a dozen people left on the floor, most of them – including Nikolai and Enzo - needing urgent attention. Two of the police officers attempted to discover from witnesses exactly what had occurred and meanwhile another group of officers retrieved two handguns and hustled two handcuffed suspects away into the waiting police van.

At the same time, the injured victims were quickly assessed and given first aid and most of them, including Aldanov and Endo, were carried gently out to the street and rushed away to the waiting ambulances which sped away to the emergency services department of the city's main hospital.

CHAPTER 2

IT ALL STARTED IN PORTSMOUTH

It was just a week later, on a Friday afternoon, when a very pensive and confused Samantha Lord was being driven back from the CIA headquarters in Langley, Virginia, to the Falls Church apartment of her new office friend Jennifer Goss. The trees along the parkway towards Washington were resplendent in their autumn colours but the Virginia scenery was not uppermost in Samantha's mind. She had just ended the most exhilarating months of her 32 years and yet she was feeling very apprehensive.

"This must be your first Fall in this part of the country," said Jennifer, abruptly interrupting Samantha's thoughts. "The trees here are pretty good but how about a trip out to Skyline Drive over the weekend – it is really spectacular there?"

"Oh yes, I have heard about it," replied Samantha. "That would be lovely if you can spare the time."

As Jennifer weaved her way through the busy traffic at the Falls Church exit and took the road to her apartment block, she continued to relate past visits to the nearby mountain area to show off the autumn colours to her family and friends. Then as they walked to the entrance lobby she paused asked thoughtfully: "Are you okay, Sam?"

"Yes, I'm fine thanks, but just a bit tired," came the reply. "Do you mind if I have a quiet evening – and maybe just take a rest for a while?"

"Sure thing," said Jennifer. "I understand." And she put an arm around Samantha as she went to the room which her friend had kindly provided for her first few weeks as a newly trained operative with the CIA. A week earlier, she had discovered a suitable apartment to rent in the same area, but she decided not to pursue the opportunity when she received the unexpected and exciting news that her first assignment was to spend a few months based in Japan. Meanwhile, she was sharing an office with Jennifer, who was an experienced member of the operational team at Langley, and they had got along famously. So she had been relieved and pleased by the offer of a spacious and comfortable room in Jennifer's apartment which saved her the trouble of setting up her own home in the area until her return from Japan, as well as the advantage of sharing the morning and evening car ride to and from headquarters.

She also began to recognise that everything that was happening to her was probably part of a grand plan for her new career. She had realised by now that nothing was just coincidental at the CIA. This included what at first seemed to be a "throwaway" comment from Bob Smithers, the Deputy Director (Operations), at the end of her briefing in his office that same afternoon.

He had been reviewing her first few weeks as a full member of his operations team and seemed pleased by her efforts. He then went on to explain that it had been decided to give her some new field experiences by going to Japan for a few weeks to work with the small CIA team based at the Tokyo embassy. This had come as a pleasant surprise, but there was another surprise to come.

As he wished her a good weekend and just as she was leaving his office, he nonchalantly told her: "By the way, Sam, your friend Tom in London has told us that there is a new defence department attache at the Russian Embassy in Tokyo – name of Aldanov."

Samantha paused, taken aback by this apparently casual but hugely significant comment. The office door had closed behind her and her mind was racing as she walked back to the office she was sharing. Unsure about the true reasons behind these farewell words, she decided to say nothing more for the time being.

The "Tom" who had been mentioned so casually by the American Deputy Director was Tom Spencer, his regular operational contact at the MI5 headquarters in London. They were just two of the very few people on both sides of the Atlantic who knew exactly how Samantha had become one of the CIA operatives in the USA. The Official Secrets Act and sealed documents in the UK's Home Office archives ensured that the extraordinary events of the previous two years remained undisclosed, despite determined efforts by the media.

It had all started when Marina Peters, a civilian assistant based in the busy communications department of the Royal Navy headquarters in Portsmouth, became dissatisfied with her personal life and started to search dating websites in the evenings at her Southsea flat. Eventually, she was attracted by the photo of an attractive officer in the Russian navy who ticked all the right boxes. They discovered two significant interests in common – the navy and Marina's ancestry as the grand-daughter of a couple who had emigrated from Russia to London in the 1930's. One of her dreams was to find a way to visit the area of Southern Russia which had once been their home and as they exchanged on-line messages, she began to think that maybe this new contact would be a step towards achieving that ambition.

Over a period of several weeks, her friendship with Nikolai Aldanov, her "Russian Lieutenant", blossomed into a long-range romance and she was thrilled when he told her that his ship would soon be calling into Portsmouth. They eventually met at the dockside and became even closer as they toured the city together and eventually returned to Marina's flat after dinner in a nearby Italian restaurant. She was happy, enchanted by her on-line date in person – was this "the real thing?" she asked herself.

What she did not suspect was that he was a spy from Russia's GRU headquarters in Moscow, who had used his skills to create this promising source of information from within the British navy. Neither did she suspect that their on-line exchanges were being monitored by the British intelligence service and that every moment of their special day in Portsmouth was being closely observed by MI5 agents. And they were making love in Marina's bedroom when the agents eventually broke into the flat, interrupted their romantic evening and arrested them both.

At the police station, the lengthy questioning of each of them was led by Tom Spencer of MI5 together with Portsmouth's CID chief. The next day, Aldanov was charged with espionage and seeking to obtain information from a Royal Navy source. However, it was agreed that Marina had not revealed any confidential information during their on-line exchanges and that her most important role would be as the main witness in the high-profile trial of a Russian spy. While Aldanov was on remand in a high security prison in London to await the trial, the story of Marina and the Russian Lieutenant became front page news.

The press, TV and radio media were all eager to interview Marina and it was discovered that officials from the Russian Embassy in London also wanted to find her – either to influence her evidence or to prevent her from being a witness. A senior Russian diplomat tried to get the support of Marina's father, now a successful businessman in London, and two Russian agents were sent to Portsmouth in a determined attempt to track her down.

But Tom Spencer at MI5 was two steps ahead. Marina was taken to a "safe house" in London while she prepared her evidence and was looked after by his experienced assistant, Patricia Wells. They were both increasingly impressed by Marina's capabilities and intelligence, and they began to consider whether she had the potential to work for the secret service – "when this is all over"? As the interest of both the press and the Russians became more intense, Tom called his contact at the CIA in Langley, Virginia, to explain the situation and they agreed that to keep her safe until the trial she would travel secretly to the USA – and where better than to the CIA's remote training establishment in Florida to take a Russian language course.

Typical of the secret services of both countries, this subterfuge went exactly as planned but after only three weeks there came a surprise development. A British diplomat serving at the embassy in Moscow was under house arrest for allegedly travelling outside the city boundaries without permission and photographing defence facilities. The Foreign Office saw an opportunity to avoid an embarrassing trial in Moscow and through third party channels, arranged a secretive "spy swap". A bewildered Aldanov was taken from his prison cell and flown out early one morning from the RAF station in Ruislip to a military airfield in Finland; and at about the same time, the British diplomat in Moscow was feeling fearful as he was woken very early by armed officers and driven from his flat to a nearby airfield with no explanation. To his great surprise and relief, he also arrived in Finland where a low-key exchange procedure took place. Documents were signed and handed over by the respective government officers and just a few hours later, he could hardly believe it when he was back with his family in London.

The legal process against Aldanov in the UK was abandoned and a surprised Marina was flown back from the USA to London, disappointed to leave sunny Florida so soon. She was taken to a government-owned flat in London to rest and then on the day after her arrival, she was driven to the MI5 headquarters for a debriefing with Tom Spencer and Patricia Wells. They explained the new developments, including the Russian spy swap, and she was relieved to know that her evidence would not be needed after all. They went on to discuss their ideas of a future career for Marina with MI5 and by mid-day, with her mind still spinning, she tried to relax at last as she was able to telephone her parents in Putney. They were understandably relieved to hear her voice again and were anxious to see her to explain what had been happening since she was front page news. She took the underground train to join them for an emotional, long lunch together. Her parents listened in amazed silence as she explained her meeting with the Russian, the prospect of a trial and then her unexpected trip to America. Later, as she was being driven by her father to Clapham Junction station for a train back to Portsmouth, he told her how he had been harassed by people at the Russian embassy wanting to locate her – and he was actually grateful that he had no idea where she was. At Portsmouth station, she took a taxi to her familiar first floor flat overlooking the Solent. "Home at last", she sighed as she put her key in the lock.

After such an extraordinary six weeks away, she slowly began to settle in again and went to the nearby store for some essential groceries, but with much still circling around in her mind. Her neighbour interrupted her as she entered her apartment, but Marina was in no mood to talk. And then she remembered to go down to the lobby again to collect the inevitable accumulation of mail from her overflowing personal mailbox. Eventually she began to relax with a cup of coffee and quickly scanned through the pile of letters. Firstly, she selected a large buff envelope which looked like it might be something important – perhaps from the Navy?

As she pulled it open, the envelope suddenly unleashed a flood of white powder over her hands, arms and face. Her eyes were tingling and she was sufficiently alarmed to quickly grab her phone to dial 999. Through her groans of increasing pain, she was just able to give her address and ask for urgent help.

Within a few minutes, the lady in the neighbouring flat was alarmed by the noise as two members of the emergency services arrived and forced open the door of Marina's flat where they found her unconscious on the floor. The mysterious white powder made them cautious and one of them tried to check her breathing. They were assessing their next move when a police officer arrived. He quickly assessed the situation and advised them to touch nothing and await the arrival of a doctor who had been called from the local hospital. More police were soon on the scene to move the anxious neighbours away from the second-floor lobby area and advised them that this was a crime scene. The doctor confirmed that he believed the white powder was a poisonous substance and told the emergency team to put on protective clothing before trying to get the victim to the hospital urgently.

Suitably protected, the two men used a body bag from their ambulance to carefully wrap the woman before putting her on a stretcher to get down the stairs to the ambulance, watched by other bewildered residents of the neighbouring flats. Meanwhile, the CID chief had arrived on the scene to assess the evidence and he confirmed that the familiar address indicated that the victim was most likely to be Marina Peters who he had interviewed at some length during the "Russian Lieutenant" inquiries just a few weeks earlier.

At Portsmouth hospital, the senior medical staff went into a major alert mode and immediately moved the patient into an isolation unit. After getting further advice from experts at the Porton Down research establishment, they agreed that from the limited available information, including the Russian links, Ricin poisoning was the probable cause of the problem. When the CID chief heard this news, he quickly decided that the two Russian 'spooks' who had travelled to Portsmouth a month earlier to find Marina Peters, were the prime suspects. They had been identified at the time as known agents from photographs taken surrepticiously by his officers and he quickly authorised arrest warrants to be issued with their names for "attempted murder." Widespread inquiries began and it was soon discovered by Scotland Yard that the same two men had both flown from Heathrow to Moscow that same morning, no doubt aware of what would be discovered on Marina's return to Portsmouth.

Meanwhile, Tom Spencer at MI5 in London was in contact with his opposite number, Bob Smithers, at the CIA headquarters in the USA about the suspicion of Ricin poisoning – a top priority with the security services of both nations in view of recent incidents. He was told that American researchers had been working on a new antidote for Ricin which had not yet been tested on an active case. However, at present, this treatment was held only in Washington for further tests but it had also been supplied to specialists at the American Military Hospital at Landstuhl in Germany, which had to be prepared for any eventuality in case of terrorism activities in Europe or the Middle East.

Tom's creative mind worked overtime! He was told by the Portsmouth hospital that Marina's condition was critical with a 50-50 survival chance at best, and so he developed an audacious plan. This was to secretly fly Marina to Germany that night by medivac plane but at the same time to announce her death and arrange a "fake funeral". This, he explained to Bob Smithers in Washington, would be a win-win operation – if the antidote was successful and Marina survived with all her faculties, they would have a potential new member of their team with the advantage of a completely new identity. On the other hand, if she could not be saved, then nothing further need ever be said and at least the scientists would have learned something about their new procedure.

Marina's "funeral" went ahead in the Portsmouth dockyard naval church with family, friends and Navy personnel present. Then, following the cremation and as her ashes were being scattered into the Solent from the sea wall, a stranger stepped forward and he cast a single red rose into the rippling water. He handed a card to the navy chaplain who paused and then read it to the gathered mourners: *"Farewell Marina. It was not supposed to end like this. RIP – your Russian Lieutenant."*

Tom Spencer had travelled to Portsmouth that day to merge discretely with the mourners and he recognised the stranger with the flower as a senior diplomat from the Russian embassy in London. As they all left the funeral ceremony to walk back to the nearby car park, the stranger was confronted by the MI5 man and a police officer and arrested for being an accessory to the murder of Marina Peters. He was discretely driven away to the local police station and formally charged. In spite of pleas from the Russian embassy in London for diplomatic immunity, and outrage from Moscow, the diplomat appeared in the Crown Court a month later and was sentenced to eight years in jail.

CHAPTER 3

CREATING AGENT "SAM"

T om Spencer's imaginative plan moved ahead. The treatment programme in Germany was slow to show results, but the specialists persevered with each stage and they eventually began to report gradual successful results. Tom and his assistant Patricia Wells were able to check on progress during their visits to the slowly recovering Marina at Landstuhl and as she regained her strength, American and British psychologists confirmed her readiness to face a new future. The next stages of the plan were implemented one step at a time.

It was agreed that to help her to adopt a new persona and leave her past behind, it would be easier to train her for a new life and career in the USA instead of in Britain with its reminders of the past. And so, when the time was right, accompanied by her new MI5 friend Patricia, she was flown by the US Air force from Germany to Washington where she became a new recruit for the CIA with a new name invented by Tom Spencer – she would become Samantha Lord.

She was given her new documentation as an American citizen and after an initial welcome at the

CIA headquarters in Langley, Virginia, Samantha and Patricia were taken the next day to the military medical research establishment in Washington DC where the research team which had developed the Ricin antidote were delighted to see their 'human guinea pig'. They carried out a series of tests to confirm the efficacy of their treatment programme and agreed that the results were positive. After a few days to settle in at Langley, and as Samantha was gaining in confidence, ready to begin a full programme of training for her new career, Patricia was able to wish her friend well and return to London.

The programme continued at a secret CIA centre in California where a team of Hollywood-trained experts created the new Samantha - and even Patricia could not recognise her when she paid another visit a few weeks later. Next came a full-on schedule including field training with the US military, experience with handguns and new secret communications devices, lectures on global politics and briefings from experienced agents on their varied experiences. At the end, Samantha was a new American citizen, fully documented and ready for her first mission as a rookie operative for 'The Company'.

Her first assignment was to travel alone to Guadalajara in Mexico as a tourist and collect some important secret documents from a CIA informant about the future plans of a drug cartel. When she went to pick up the file, her arrival at his home was spotted by watching members of the gang, but she managed to escape safely from a rear door as a gun fight took place at the front. Then, a few weeks later, she was assigned to go to Toronto to search for a Russian cyber operation which was interfering with government communications in the USA. She successfully discovered the location and identified the individuals from the city's large Russian community who were involved. To preserve her anonymity, she returned to Washington just before the illicit operation was raided by the Canadian police and security services and the Russians cyber experts were detained.

It was during her return train journey to Washington, that her concentration on making a success in her new life was suddenly shattered by reading news from England in the New York Times of yet another Ricin attack. This time it was at a ceremony in Portsmouth dockyard to unveil a memorial to Marina Peters and the victim was none other than her MI5 friend, Patricia Wells. It was reported that a Russian agent had gained access to the event by wearing a stolen Royal Navy uniform and had fired a Ricin pellet into the thigh of his victim before escaping in the crowd.

Using her mobile phone and a special protected line, a desperately worried Samantha was able to contact Tom Spencer in London from the train for the reassuring news that although Patricia was in hospital she was recovering and receiving excellent treatment. She was relieved to hear this news from someone she trusted, and she decided not to mention it to anyone when she returned to Langley. Instead, she would focus on the success of her first two assignment, to Mexico and Canada, which had led to the decision to give her the further international experience by working with the small CIA team based at the American embassy in Japan.

At her Friday debriefing with Bob Smithers, he told her that she would have a full week of preparation with the East Asian team at headquarters, starting the following Monday and that she should be ready to depart a few days later.

And it was then, as she was leaving his office for a restful weekend, that Bob had casually mentioned the name of Aldanov!

CHAPTER 4
NOT JUST A COINCIDENCE

S amantha was resting on her bed back at Jennifer's apartment on that Friday evening, deep in confused thoughts about her new life and the 'bombshell' comment by the CIA chief about Aldanov, together with the latest news from London about Patricia, when her new American friend knocked the door and brought a long, cold drink to the bedside table. "Can I get you anything else – maybe something to eat?" she asked.

"That's so kind," replied Samantha and just for a moment, she realised how much she would really like to be able to share her thoughts with her new friend. But then her new reality took over and she replied: "Not just now - but I will come and join you a bit later if you don't mind."

As Jennifer left the room with a warm and understanding smile, Samantha began to wonder just how much her new friend already knew? The story of Marina Peters and her Russian Lieutenant, the Ricin poisoning and the funeral had been covered fully by the media in the UK and no doubt elsewhere in the world including the USA. But she had been reassured by her new Director that her subsequent reincarnation remained a state secret, known only by a few very senior people on both sides of the Atlantic.

However, the details of Aldanov's spy-swap, the trial of the Russian diplomat and then the second Ricin attack in Portsmouth had also made big news. Samantha had been able to read these reports on her computer in quiet moments - with very confused and mixed feelings. As she read the details of these events, she could still hardly believe what had happened to her. She certainly appreciated the remarkable opportunity she had been given to start a completely new life, but… and there were so many "buts" in her thoughts.

She wondered what had happened to her lovely parents back in England after they had been at the mock funeral? How was Patricia and was she still making a good recovery? Had all her friends in Portsmouth forgotten her? What happened to Nikolai after that special day they shared? What had he been doing back in Russia? Why was he now going to Japan? And was this just a coincidence? No – there are no coincidences in this strange world she now inhabited! Did she make the right decision to start this new life and new career? And on the other hand, what was the alternative? She was really lucky to be alive at all, and actually enjoying the new experiences.

All of these thoughts and more crowded into her confused mind and she longed to share them with someone. But Jennifer was a very new friend. As an experienced CIA employee, she would be familiar with keeping things confidential, but the extraordinary story of how Marina had become Samantha might test her resolve when talking to other long-time CIA friends. And with her loyalty to The Company, she might even begin to question Samantha's commitment if she revealed the story of her past life – and even her family's Russian connection.

So, no - she would remain strong. She recognised that she too had now signed on to the CIA code and would not risk letting down those who had enabled her to have this exciting new challenge and a new life after the enemy had tried to kill her.

Then her thoughts returned to Patricia, who had become a real friend through the most difficult times, and she was also one of the handful of people who actually knew the whole story. However, she would be patient and wait until she could go to London to visit her special friend for the heart-to-heart chat she was craving. But when would that be? She resolved to speak to Tom Spencer as soon as possible to discover the latest news and hopefully arrange a way to go to London.

Samantha's mind began to clear. She quickly washed her face, changed into a relaxed t-shirt and jeans and went to find Jennifer who was in the sitting room reading the Washington Post. "Hi and sorry if I have kept you waiting", she said cheerfully. "So when shall we go to see those Fall colours on Skyline Drive?"

"Let's start making some plans," came the warm and friendly reply. "You look rested now, so let's put on a movie and have a quiet supper – I have some salads waiting in the kitchen with a bottle of Chardonnay".

CHAPTER 5
RUSSIA'S REPRISAL

I n "The Aquarium", the modern headquarters of Russia's GRU in the suburbs of Moscow, Yuri Bortsov was enjoying his recent promotion to become chief of the 5th Directorate. He had been a highly regarded young science graduate, recruited and trained as a secret service agent during Putin's regime as the head of GRU. During overseas postings to embassies in Europe and Africa, Bortsov had been credited with successfully recruiting valuable informants before returning to Moscow with promotion to the administration team as head of the section developing and testing new cyber-technologies.

Now, after an impressive three years as a manager, this fit and active official in his late forties had been chosen for yet another important promotion with the challenge of restoring confidence in the 5th Directorate after the embarrassment of "the Aldanov affair". His new task was managing the recruitment, training and operations of the government's entire international spy network.

His predecessor, together with his deputy, had both been quietly moved to other duties in the defence ministry after the publicity around the world for many weeks about the failed attempt by agent Nikolai Aldanov to use an on-line dating site to make contact with Marina Peters, who worked for the British navy in Portsmouth. The embarrassed leaders in the Kremlin decided that he had not been properly directed as he undertook an assignment to pose as a Russian naval officer to exchange messages with Marina and establish a significant new contact. He had been assigned to join a warship which was scheduled to visit Portsmouth to meet her in person. But in what apparently became a romantic relationship, they were followed during their day together and were arrested in her flat at night by British security services. Aldanov was charged with espionage and held in jail awaiting a trial.

He became known in the press headlines as "The Russian Lieutenant" but before the case came to court, the GRU directors were relieved when he was returned to Russia as part of a "spy swap" with a British diplomat, then under house arrest for allegedly contravening travel restrictions. However, two Russian agents had already been assigned to find Marina Peters, who would have been the key witness in the trial of Aldanov. The agents had failed to locate her and were later accused by the police of leaving a package of Ricin poison in the mailbox at Marina's home, which apparently led to her death and then the widely reported naval funeral.

The Russian government was angered by this series of public embarrassments and responded by expelling 10 British diplomats from Moscow and sending strong letters of protest to the Foreign Office. The challenge faced by Bortsov was to rebuild confidence in the reputation and operations of the GRU and he began by reorganising his senior intelligence team. He urged them to focus on greater professionalism, the verification of overseas assignments and stronger central control. He gave the files on "The Aldanov Case" to one of his trusted lieutenants, Petrov, to study, together with the news that the man himself had been moved safely away from GRU and was now assigned to diplomatic duties in Japan.

Alongside his other assignments, Petrov decided to start by tracking the activities of the man identified in the files as Marina Peters' spymaster, a senior MI5 officer named Tom Spencer. Also on his list were her father, Victor Peters, and her contacts in the British navy. Using the GRU's research resources in Moscow and London, he discovered more information about the family's Russian background and Marina's career before she joined the Royal Navy's headquarters in Portsmouth. He also became suspicious that Tom Spencer had developed a separate secret plan to use Marina's knowledge as a way to build up more information about the movements of foreign navies than was available through existing sources. She might have been a more important cog in the security wheel than originally thought?

After a few weeks, Petrov went to his boss with a new plan. "I think we should do more than expelling a few British diplomats," he said. "If we are looking for a meaningful reprisal, we should consider targeting the British spymaster."

This got Bortszov's full attention. "Tell me more," he said, eagerly.

"We have discovered details about an event in Portsmouth dockyard next week to unveil a memorial plaque to the woman Peters," he continued. "She was obviously more important that we thought, because some of the top navy brass will be there as well as her family and we have information that the MI5 man Spencer will be there too. As you know, the Brits are sentimental people but because it is inside the dockyard there will not be much security at the actual event. So I have been working with our agents in London who have done a thorough recce of the location. They have developed a plan to kidnap a naval man leaving the dockyard on the previous evening and use his uniform for one of them to go into the dockyard early in next morning. He can easily merge with all the routine activity there until it is time to mingle with the group attending the plaque unveiling. We will provide him with photos to enable identification of the MI5 man Spencer and he can use a Ricin pellet to finish the job. Then it should not be difficult for our man to slip away unnoticed in the pandemonium which will follow. You can be sure that our guys know the ropes and they can probably take it all in their stride. What do you think?"

"Good work, Petrov," said the boss. "Does our London team think they can handle the logistics of transport and getting away afterwards?"

"All worked out," came the confident reply. "Leave it to me and just watch for the British headlines next week."

"Sounds too good to be true" said Bortsov after a few moments of thought. "So let me get clearance from the minister and hopefully I will give you the go ahead. Good luck."

A week later, he saw the headlines in the British media about the unveiling of the plaque – and the coverage had been overwhelmed by details of another Russian Ricin attack in Portsmouth. This time the victim was described as "a female government officer", who was there as one of Marina's friends. Then there were details of how a British sailor had been kidnapped for his uniform, which was used to gain access to the dockyard to carry out the attack. And the reports went on to describe the subsequent arrest of the two Russian agents thought to have been responsible on a Eurostar train to Brussels. But there was no mention of Tom Spencer or MI5.

"So what happened?" asked Bortsov, when he called his senior team together to review the matter. "Was your man Spencer there or not?"

"I guess we will never know, or at least not until we can de-brief the agent with the Ricin gun," said a disappointed Petrov. "And that may take a few years. But everything else went as planned and we certainly showed that we can hit back and no-one knows who the real target was."

"Okay – so seven out of ten for that operation, I guess", was the assessment by the chief. "You say that no-one knows about the real target. Don't be too sure. The top people at MI5 will have it worked out for certain. So keep your eyes on the UK situation and the Peters family. I have a feeling that there is more to come on this one."

CHAPTER 6
PREPARING FOR JAPAN

A relaxed weekend and a sight-seeing trip to Virginia was exactly what Samantha needed to prepare her for the week ahead. The Fall colours on Skyline Drive were spectacular and the viewing areas were very busy with weekend sightseers with their cameras. They also visited one of the Civil War battle museums which gave her new insights into American history, followed by a wonderful seafood dinner with lobster from the Chesapeake Bay. On Sunday they pottered around the shops in Georgetown and afterwards Samantha was introduced to the tradition of watching a movie with a bucket of popcorn. Then, on Monday morning, rested and back at the office in Langley, she found a quiet moment to make the important call to Tom Spencer in London on his direct line.

"How nice to hear your voice again," he began. "But you don't sound very American yet. I've been hearing good things about your work there and it sounds like you are enjoying it?"

"Yes, I am," she replied. "And I really appreciate all you did to make this happen. But I have several things I want to ask you about. First of all, did you know that

I am being assigned to work in Japan to get some more experience and that I will probably be heading that way in the next week?"

"Yes, I did," said Tom. "Bob Smithers shared that with me and it sounds like a great idea. I guess you have never been there – it should be really interesting."

Samantha then asked: "Yes, but this is the Russian thing coming round again, isn't it? I really thought we had agreed to put all that into the past. Did you know that Nikolai Aldanov has just been posted to the Russian Embassy in Tokyo. That's not just a coincidence, is it?"

"I guess not," said Tom, rather cautiously. "We heard about this on the grapevine a couple of weeks ago and I shared the news with Bob when he was deciding where to assign you next and it just seemed to make some sort of sense – we never know when our past experiences are going to come in handy. And anyway, it is really hard to get away from what you call the Russian thing. You will find out in time that about half of everything we do in this business has something to do with Russia".

Samantha was thoughtful. She had come to trust Tom more than anyone else, so she said nothing, as he continued: "The sort of work you get involved with in Japan will be a matter for you and the CIA head of station in Tokyo to work out. And it will be very much up to you, of course, because I promise you that they will not know anything about your Russian interests in the past."

Samantha mumbled a few words of agreement but made no comment and Tom went on: "I realise that this might sound like a bit of a fix-up, but remember that only Bob and myself know about you and Aldanov and we decided that it just could be a valuable connection for you to make at some stage – who knows?"

"Well, I am getting used to surprises in this business," she replied as cheerfully as she could. "I guess it goes with the territory and I will think some more about it. But there's another important thing on my mind and that is Patricia. How is she?"

"She is still in hospital," said Tom. "But I am pleased to say that her recovery is coming along as well as we could have expected. I'm afraid it looks like she has lost some of her mobility at this stage and she may be in a wheelchair for the foreseeable future. But she is having the best possible treatment. The good news is that she is as bright and cheerful as ever and she wants to return to the office as soon as possible. It could have easily been a lot worse."

"That's a relief, I must say," said Samantha with a sigh, and then went on: "Look, Tom, you know she was very important in my being here at all and I have an idea. If I can get the people here to route me via London on my way to Tokyo, do you think I could visit you and Patricia?"

Tom Spencer was relieved to move on from the subject of Aldanov and said it sounded like a good plan and that he would try to work it out. "Let me discuss your travel arrangements with Bob Smithers later and he will let you know what can be done," he added.

He reassured her that they would talk again in a day or two, so Samantha decided to delay asking him about seeing her parents until the next conversation.

Her programme for the next two days was mainly a series of briefings from the senior CIA managers on the subject of Japan, including the organization of the various staff based at the Tokyo embassy and the issues she could expect to find there. She was surprised to learn that although it might seem at first sight to be one of the quieter regions for the work of The Company – the name they all used for the CIA - Japan was also the operational base for over 40,000 American military personnel and their families. There were also several air force bases and frequent visits to Japanese ports by the US Navy. It was, she was told, the centre of America's western Pacific operations and strategically, it was just a few dozen miles from the shores of Eastern Russia and an important Russian naval base.

This was all new information for Samantha and the references to Russian bases certainly got her attention, especially when at another briefing one of the Asian experts described a long-term dispute concerning Japan's Northern Territories. The "geography lesson" described how this was a largely barren group of islands stretching from Japan's northerly Hokkaido island towards the Baring Sea and the Arctic and it was close to one of Russia's most easterly peninsulas. These islands had been occupied by the Soviet forces during World War Two and renamed as the Kuril Islands.

Then one of the CIA's Asian political experts described how the dispute between Japan and Russia over the Kurils had continued since 1945. Successive Japanese governments had raised the issue of the territorial ownership of the islands at the highest levels, but without making any progress, in spite of American backing. The key issue over restoring any of the island territories to Japan was an undertaking required by

Russia not to permit its use by the US military - which, not surprisingly, Japan's close Pacific ally was unwilling to accept. There were two other critical matters to be aware of. Firstly, aerial reconnaissance showed that the Russians were installing rocket bases on the islands; and secondly, owning the territorial waters around the islands gave the Russian navy and other shipping more direct access to the Pacific Ocean, particularly during the winter months.

Samantha quickly recognised that there were more potential issues for the Tokyo embassy to follow than she had been expecting. But her intense concentration on her Japan briefings was interrupted at the end of the third day when she found a "strictly confidential" message on her desk from Bob Smithers' assistant. It instructed her to contact the travel office as soon as possible the next day and to be prepared to fly to London on the following Sunday. There was also a hand-written note from Bob Smithers suggesting that she should also call Tom Spencer again as soon as possible.

CHAPTER 7

A STOPOVER IN LONDON

At the riverside HQ of MI5 in London, Tom Spencer and two members of his operations team began to make plans for a confidential visit to London by an important, unnamed visitor from the CIA. This was not an unusual requirement and he assigned one of his senior staff to welcome the visitor at Heathrow and take her to the VIP centre to deal with the usual formalities.

"By the way, she is an attractive American lady", he added, before advising them that she should be driven with her luggage to a familiar safe house in Hammersmith where Tom himself would be waiting for her. Arrangements then needed to be made for her to stay there for up to 48 hours with one of their special housekeepers taking care of her personal needs. He told his two agents that they should remain on standby and protection duties throughout the visit, but that he would take care of the details of the visitor's programme.

When Samantha called from Washington, she confirmed that she was booked on a BA flight from Washington, arriving in London at about 10am on the following Monday morning and that she had been given an open ticket for an onward flight to Tokyo on a date to be confirmed.

"Good – it seems to be working as you hoped," he told her. "I gather from Patricia that I may not recognise you when you arrive, but I am really looking forward to seeing you again. And I have already arranged a time for you two to get together. You have a lot to catch up on. By the way, one of my team will meet your flight and bring you to meet me."

"That's sounds lovely," said Samantha, before adding rather tentatively, "There's one more thing and this may be asking too much, but do you think there is some way I can see my parents again?"

"Ah, yes, of course," replied Tom rather cautiously. "I do understand, but I'm sorry to say that I have some rather sad news to share with you. Last winter, your poor father had a heart attack and passed away soon afterwards. He had been harassed by the Russians quite relentlessly after your, shall I say, disappearance. I think they thought that after losing you, he would be vulnerable and would weaken in his determination not to help them in any way. But as far as we know he stayed firm and I am quite sure that neither they nor your father had any inkling about what really happened."

"Oh dear, that's really sad," said a tearful Samantha. "What about my mother?"

"We did stay in very discrete contact with both your parents over the last couple of years, as well as your uncle Andrew who has continued to run the business," said Tom. "But the last I heard was that your mother decided to return to her family home in Northern Ireland and that she is now living with her sister somewhere outside of Belfast. I am sorry not to have kept you in the picture, but in the circumstances, it seemed to be better not to interrupt your progress in the States. Anyway, let's talk some more about this when we get together next week."

"Yes, please," replied a very subdued Samantha. "So when can I see Patricia?"

"Don't worry - that's all fixed," said Tom. "You can have lots of time together."

Samantha's remaining days in Washington kept her busy as her travel plans were finalised and documents were supplied for all her needs in London and Tokyo. She worked on her itinerary with the travel department, including the options for her onward flight to Japan – and of course there was the usual challenge of packing her travel bags for what could be several months away, with valuable help and advice from the well-travelled Jennifer. Early on Sunday evening, the car arrived on schedule to take her to Dulles airport and the British Airways flight in the comfort of a business class cocoon seat. After enjoying the dinner service and a glass of wine, she relaxed for couple of hours' sleep and then it was time for breakfast before the arrival formalities suddenly reminded her of the reality that she was back in London again.

"Miss Lord?" asked the flight attendant as the plane taxied towards the terminal, interrupting her thoughts. Samantha nodded and was told quietly to be prepared to leave the aircraft first because she was being met at the gangway by VIP services. A few minutes after the plane came to a halt, a smart young man was waiting at the aircraft door to take her hand baggage and escort her through the terminal walkways to the VIP lounge where she was welcomed by a man who introduced himself as Keith Harmison from Tom Spencer's office. They talked about the weather and had coffee together while the man from BA went back to the main building to collect her two suitcases which, he explained to her surprise, had been given special VIP tags in Washington.

Keith then signed some documents with an official from the immigration department and explained that a government car was standing by to take them both to a house in West London where Tom Spencer would be waiting – and Samantha, bemused by the star treatment she was receiving, decided to relax and go with the flow…

As the car cruised along the M4 towards West London, she realised it was nearly two years since she had last been in England. But it all looked so familiar – it was even raining. On the way, Keith explained that they were heading for a government rest house, used by special visitors to MI5 and also as a safe haven when needed. When they arrived, she could see that it was an anonymous Victorian-era detached house like many others in the area. Keith led her inside, carrying her luggage, and in the front sitting room, on his own, was the familiar and friendly sight of Tom Spencer. He stepped back as he studied her from head to toe and said: "So welcome, Samantha. Whatever happened to Marina?" Then he moved forward and greeted her with a hug and indicated a comfortable chair, asking: "Are you tired after your flight?"

"I'm okay thanks", she replied. "I had some sleep during the night but a cup of coffee would be nice."

Tom asked Keith to find the housekeeper and arrange coffee for them all and then told him to wait in the next room for further instructions. Turning back to Samantha, he continued: "Well, it is really great to see you at last – or should I say see the new you. But you really are looking terrific, if I may say so. It has been quite a while and so much has happened to you and to us here in London. I don't really know where to start."

Samantha shook her head, feeling rather overwhelmed as she agreed with him and was not sure what to say next – but coffee arrived and provided a few moments to think. When they were on their own again, she said: "I really want to thank you for all that you have done for me. I know I am very lucky to have survived that dreadful experience in Portsmouth and the treatment I had from the Americans in Germany was just fantastic. And now I have a whole new life – as an American. It is really hard to believe, but I have not had much time to think lately because my life is so busy… and exciting, too."

"That's great," said Tom. "I always knew you had the potential to fit into our business. And it seems to have worked out well for everybody."

"Except for poor Patricia," Samantha interrupted. "I was so sorry to hear what happened to her. How is she now and when can I get to see her?"

"Yes, that's part of the plan," said Tom. "As I told you in our phone call, she is making a remarkable recovery and I have arranged to take you to the rehab unit in Surrey tomorrow morning. Although she was hit by the same Ricin poison as you, the effect of the pellet fired into her thigh was very different from the white powder which you ingested. According to the medics, she has made a full recovery of her mental faculties, but she still has a physical disability affecting just the lower half of her body. Apparently, this is the result of the Ricin poisoning causing a sort of mini-stroke. They tell me that the low blood pressure led to some spinal damage and that in this case, partial paraplegia was the result. They are still working on it, but the damage has affected the movement in her legs and although she has recovered pretty well otherwise, she is still having treatment and therapy to restore her mobility".

Samantha listened carefully to this explanation, with increasing horror and through her tears, she replied: "Oh my god, that sounds just terrible. Why did they attack Patricia?"

"Well to be honest, that continues to worry me, Samantha," said Tom. "I cannot help feeling that the attack was really meant for me and that in the crowd there in the dockyard the Russian agent got it wrong. At the time, I was hanging on to Patricia in a moving group of people and he probably had to work quickly as he tried to mingle with us. Apparently, he was holding a sort of pistol concealed under a coat which was over his arm. So it is difficult to work out exactly what happened from the the security camera pictures. But as you know better than anyone, these are pretty ruthless characters and I am pretty sure I was the intended target, so I feel really bad every time I see poor Patricia. I just thank goodness it is no worse than it is."

"So what happened to the Russian?" asked Samantha "Did they catch him this time?"

Tom decided it was a good opportunity to explain the whole story, starting with the unveiling of the memorial plaque in the Dockyard in memory of Marina Peters. He described how after the ceremony, the group of about a hundred VIPs were all walking across the road to have lunch in the Boathouse restaurant when the attack took place. Samantha, now with more than a year of experiences with the CIA, was still shocked as he told her how a pair of Russian agents had managed to kidnap a Royal Navy man on his way home the previous evening, drug him and steal his uniform. One of them was then able to pass through the security gates at a busy time the next morning and merge unrecognised into all the activity in the Dockyard to carry out his mission and then slip away in the mayhem which followed.

"But yes, they did catch him, and his partner", Tom concluded. And when Samantha asked what had happened next, he went on to describe how the kidnapped sailor had recovered sufficiently to give the Portsmouth police details of the car the Russians had used. It was found later the same day at a hotel near Heathrow airport – but instead of flying out as they first suspected, it was discovered that they had taken a taxi to St. Pancras station in London to catch the next Eurostar train to Brussels. Through Interpol, their identities were passed on to the Belgian police who detained the pair as they stepped off the train and held them overnight until police officers from London arrived to detain them, charge them with attempted murder and take them back to stand trial.

With that background information, Samantha breathed a sigh of relief and asked Tom for any more news about her family. He was able to tell her that because they were considered to be at risk, after the original events in Portsmouth, his department had decided to "keep tabs" on her parents and their business activities, to keep them safe.

"The Russian embassy did in fact approach your father and his brother on a number of occasions, trying to pressure them into using the contacts they had made with the Navy in Portsmouth," he replied. "And I am sorry to say that your father became quite upset by it. We did what we could to reassure him. In fact, I spoke to him a couple of times myself and we are satisfied that neither he nor his brother did anything to help the Russians in any way. But your mother felt that all this pressure, as well as losing you, contributed to his failing health and eventually there came the heart attack. We were all so sorry and one of my colleagues – in fact the lady who actually took Patricia's job as my assistant – has spent some time helping your mother in various ways.

"But it was your uncle Andrew who was able to deal with all of your father's affairs and he also helped your mother when she decided to sell the house and move to live with her sister near Belfast – and the last we heard was that she had settled into a new life there quite well."

Samantha was weeping quietly as Tom gave her the family news and she asked: "Do you think I will ever be able to see my mother again?"

"That's hard to answer," replied Tom. "Since all the press interest in your former life died down, I think she and your father came to terms with the fact that they had lost their only daughter. So it would come as a great shock to her and maybe it could even lead her to share the news about you with someone else and this would open up a real can of worms."

"Yes, I understand that, of course", replied Samantha, realising once again how fortunate she was to have actually survived and start a whole new and exciting life. And then, gathering together the newly acquired steel in her personality as a trained secret service officer, she changed the subject and said: "Let's talk more about Patricia?"

Tom breathed a sigh of relief and was pleased to be able to start explaining the treatment which his long-serving assistant had received since the Ricin pellet incident in Portsmouth. He described how she had benefited from the experience which had been gained during the earlier poisoning and how this time, the Rare Diseases Hospital in London was geared up to take over the treatment as soon as Patricia could be transferred there. But she was on the critically ill list for several weeks and it had then been a slow recovery process taking nearly two months before she was entirely clear of the poison.

"But sadly, she has lost all mobility below the waist and still requires special care as you will see tomorrow", he concluded. And then, as he saw Samantha in tears again, he quickly added: "But she will not want to worry you, because she still has all her faculties and she is taking a special interest in all the amazing things being done these days by paraplegic patients. You only have to see the Special Olympics and the Invictus Games to understand how she is thinking, so she is being very positive. And anyway, the doctors have not yet given up hope that she can gradually regain some mobility – and she even wants to come back to work".

"That sounds a bit more cheerful" replied Samantha. "So what is the plan for tomorrow? I can't wait to see Patricia – you know how important she was to me when I ended up in hospital, and then afterwards when she came with me to America."

With that, Tom decided it was time to call out for his colleague Keith to join them from the next room and set out his plans. First, they would all walk round the corner to l'Auberge restaurant where tables had been reserved for lunch – "a quiet table for two, plus a nearby table for one where Keith can keep his eyes open while he has lunch as well." Tom said he would then need to return to his office for the rest of the day and hoped Samantha would be happy to rest in her room to recover from her flight and maybe enjoy some British TV for a change. Keith would remain at the house until he was relieved by another agent who would be on overnight duty and they would also ensure that their American guest was looked after.

He then outlined how in the morning, he would collect Samantha and drive her to the private convalescent home in Surrey, just ten miles away, to spend the morning with Patricia. Then she would be driven direct to Heathrow airport in the afternoon, to catch a flight to Tokyo where it was all arranged for an officer from the US embassy to be waiting to meet her.

Samantha listened intently, admiring the efficiency of the arrangements, as Tom added: "We have a seat booked for you on a flight leaving at 4.20 and as you have probably discovered already, it is a twelve-hour flight so with a nine hour time change. So you will arrive there at about two in the afternoon of the next day. So I'm afraid you will have double jet lag by then after your flight yesterday."

"I think you have thought of everything," she replied. "And after a good rest here tonight and a long gossip with Patricia, I am sure I will be just fine for the long flight… and excited too with Tokyo to look forward to."

Lunch was an opportunity for Samantha to chat with Tom about her experiences during the training programme at the CIA headquarters in Virginia and then her first two missions to Mexico and Canada. He was increasingly impressed, and he soon appreciated that she was sounding like a typical new agent – which confirmed his earlier views that she would be a 'good fit' in the intelligence world. But he soon had to excuse himself to return to more challenges awaiting him in his office and as they parted, he felt a special bond had developed with the woman he had created. He then left her in Keith's safe care and with a farewell hug, he confirmed that he would collect her from the house at 9.30 the next morning, with her luggage ready to go.

CHAPTER 8

NOW TWO RICIN VICTIMS

Well rested and relaxed after enjoying the comforts of the "safe house" and the attentions of the bodyguards and the successive duty housekeepers, Samantha was ready for her long-awaited reunion with Patricia Wells. But she became increasingly apprehensive as Tom Spencer drove her out of London on the A30 into the Surrey countryside to meet her friend. They had last spent time together at the CIA mansion overlooking the Pacific Ocean in California where she had completed her transformation from Marina Peters into the new Samantha Lord. And now, it was going to be a rather different "new" Patricia. How the world had changed for them both.

Tom recognised her growing concerns and reassured her that she would find her friend in good spirits as well as being equally excited about them meeting again at last. And he also added that the Home Office personnel department was looking after Patricia's needs in every way and had encouraged her to understand that her job and her future were secure. So she had no worries and should concentrate on getting well again.

He was right. As they walked into her bright, sunny room in the modern and attractive rehabilitation centre, Patricia was relaxing in a comfortable reclining chair – smiling and opening her arms towards the approaching Samantha before greeting her with a hug and warm kisses. "Well, just look at you," she said at last. "You are looking wonderful, but I am so glad I was able to see you on my trip to California or I would never have recognised you. They certainly did a marvellous job there."

"Yes, they did, and I think I am getting used to it now," said Samantha with a laugh. "But I must say that you are looking just the same as ever. I have been thinking about you so much over the past few months and I know you have a new problem to cope with, but it really looks like you are the same Patricia who helped me when I needed it most".

Tom interrupted to say he would leave the two ladies to catch up while he visited two other colleagues, also recovering from problems in the same establishment, and that he would return in a couple of hours or so to take Samantha to the airport for her flight to Tokyo… and just as he left, one of the staff in her crisp white uniform arrived with a carafe of coffee on a tray with two mugs and a plate of assorted biscuits.

As they began to relax together, it was Patricia who raised the question lingering in the minds of them both – "How extraordinary that we both became victims of the Russians and their deadly poison… and both had to experience so much lengthy medical treatment… and yet we have both survived to tell the tale."

"Yes, I guess it is Britain two and Russia nil", commented Samantha before pausing to correct herself by adding that perhaps it should be "Britain and America, two". They laughed and agreed that it was the expertise of the American medical research team which actually achieved her recovery following Tom Spencer's "amazing fake funeral plan". They agreed to give credit where it was due and then Samantha asked her friend: "So tell me more about how this rehab programme is going for you?"

Patricia then explained the details of her lack of mobility and the daily treatment she was now receiving from the expert specialists, using equipment to help her move her into and out of her wheelchair to take part in therapeutic exercises, including a daily session with expert supervision in the swimming pool. And looking ahead, she said the team believed that by using the latest technology, they would be able to have her walking unaided again. She explained how this included using a wireless implant linked to her brain that targeted stimulation of the spinal cord and leg muscles.

"The clever guys here have started preparing me for this process," she said. "They tell me that the technology is being developed in Switzerland and it has already helped three patients with spinal cord injuries to learn to walk again, just with the support of crutches or a walker at first. And I only have to look at some of the other people here to realise that anything is possible these days. Just think of the competitors at the Paralympics and then the way some of our servicemen are being rehabilitated. I remember you told me that that you saw some of this at the American hospital in Germany, too".

It became a cheerful and optimistic reunion for the two friends as they remembered past experiences and they even began to talk about working together again when Samantha's Tokyo assignment came to an end – and they speculated that maybe she could even return to work in London in some way?

"Speaking of the future, how is your love life, Sam?" asked Patricia. "You must have met some exciting Americans over the past months. Is there someone special yet?"

"I wish," replied Samantha with a sigh. "It really took me a long time to get over the Alexei thing – remember that we had been corresponding for a couple of months before we actually met and it felt like the real thing in so many ways. Even after he was arrested, I did not believe he had done anything wrong and that it would all work out in the end - that is until I woke up in that German hospital and heard what really happened. And as for Americans, they all seem so brash and uncaring – not warm and understanding and generous like your boss Tom. He was so nice as he drove me to see you today. I guess it is the English way…"

"Yes, I know what you mean," replied Patricia. "I have been working for him for five years and he is terrific. But sadly he is married to his career and because of this, he has been very successful, but in a quiet and unassuming way. And by the way, I was so sorry to hear about your father and now I gather your mother has left London to return to her roots in Ireland."

"That's what I have been told," said Samantha sadly. "But the folk in the States have helped me to come to terms with all that has happened in the past and to focus on my new future. Though one day, I do think about whether it might be possible to give my mum a big surprise… maybe one day," she added wistfully, then composing herself as she spotted Tom returning to join them.

"Sorry to break up your chat, girls, but I'm afraid it is time for me to take Samantha to the airport – duty calls, in Tokyo," he said, with a laugh.

"Good luck, Sam," said Patricia. "I was going to tell you all about the month I spent in Japan on an assignment a few years ago. Anyway, you will enjoy it once you get used to their funny ways so make the most of it and let me know how you are getting on."

They shared a tearful farewell hug and a final wave as Tom led Samantha through the door and out to his car parked near the entrance. During the 30-minute drive to Heathrow, he told her more about the challenging period which Patricia had endured during the early weeks after the incident in Portsmouth. And how difficult it had been for him since he was convinced that he had been the real target for the Ricin attack. And he added: "I cannot tell you just how proud I am of both of you."

At the airport terminal, he again used his special pass to take Samantha through to the VIP area and handed her over to an officer there who checked her passport and ticket, picked up her baggage and escorted her to the gate – pausing at the W.H Smith shop to collect a newspaper and a couple of magazines for the long flight to Tokyo.

She was woken from a deep sleep by the pilot's announcement to prepare for arrival and a reminder of the clock time in Japan. It was the afternoon of the next day and she was pleased to have been able to enjoy a few hours of sleep in her business class seat, alongside a young Japanese businessman who was thankfully small and quiet, apart from a few polite words each time the cabin services arrived. And then it was time to disembark into the crowded arrivals area of Narita airport where among the galaxy of name boards being held up in Japanese, she thankfully spotted a woman holding a sign which read simply "Samantha Lord."

CHAPTER 9

INTRODUCTION TO TOKYO

There was warm, Autumn sunshine to greet Samantha as she walked out of Tokyo's Narita airport terminal building, accompanied by Mary-Jo from the American embassy and a Japanese driver from who took charge of her two large suitcases on the baggage trolley. Samantha relaxed in the back of the luxurious limousine on the long, slow drive to the city as Mary-Jo introduced herself as an administrator at the embassy, responsible for travel arrangements. She did her best to concentrate as her new American colleague recalled her own impressions of Japan, gained as a recent newcomer herself to Tokyo and to the customs of living and travelling around the country.

"You will need to get used to all the etiquette here," she began. "It is probably quite different from anything you are expecting. Japanese people constantly bow, so you don't attempt to shake hands, but just bow back. And the more senior the other person is, the lower you need to go".

They laughed together at this as Mary-Jo continued: "But they are usually friendly and helpful and complete strangers will approach you if you're looking lost and even go out of their way to give you directions. You will sometimes find that the locals are even happy to take you to your destination and with no hassle – just a smile and a bow. Another thing that surprised me was to find that It is such a male dominated society. The men work longer hours and often go drinking afterwards and most women tend to stay at home".

Samantha realized that this background information was going to be important to her as she settled into her new surroundings. She had already recognised the good manners of everyone in the crowds around her at the airport and now in the countryside, as they were driving through heavy but fast-moving traffic towards the city, she noted to her surprise that vehicles were driving on the left.

As they travelled, the talkative Mary-Jo continued: "I have only been here a month myself, but you will soon discover that footwear is very important – and not just what you are wearing. It's common practice to take shoes off when arriving at a home, hotel or even a restaurant as soon as you are across the threshold. You are then given a pair of indoor slippers to wear – these can be anything from crocs to Japanese style wooden flip flops. They usually come as large, medium or small rather than exact sizes so you can find yourself in a pair that are a too loose or too tight".

They laughed together again at this description and had another chuckle when Mary-Jo added: "And by the way, if you are using a shared toilet anywhere, you are expected to change shoes at the toilet door, but you can't help but wonder how many other pairs of feet have been wearing the same pair of toilet slippers".

To Samantha's surprise, Mary-Jo then continued to pursue the same subject as she continued: "By the way, this country takes its toilets seriously, and unlike back in the US, you will find that public facilities appear just when you need them, and often when you don't. If you are wandering around a city centre, you are never far from the nearest loo, and what's more they are always clean and well-maintained. And by the way, the toilet itself can be another surprise! The Japanese version in hotels and restaurants often looks like a work of science. Before you have even closed the door, up pops the lid automatically ready to welcome you and with a lovely, heated seat. Then there is a control panel with an array of buttons and an information board to guide you through the features and icons. So allow extra time for your first few visits, not least because you will want to sit and study it all".

Samantha wondered what was coming next in this unexpected welcome and realized that she was hearing anything except the information she was expecting, such as the work of the Embassy. She learned how to enjoy miso soup, tofu and a lot of raw fish in sushi and sashimi. She should not be surprised to find that smoking is still allowed in restaurants and bars and that, unlike in the USA, tipping was not required at all – "in fact it can often cause confusion and embarrassment if you try". Next in Mary-Jo's briefing came taxis – "They are very clean and smart and they all have rear doors on the left-hand side of the car which open automatically and can take you by surprise", she added. "And the drivers usually wear smart suits and white gloves".

Samantha interrupted to ask her guide about seeing more of Japan beyond Tokyo and Mary-Jo went on to encourage her to try using Ryokans if she was travelling around the country. These are traditional Japanese houses, she explained, with a lot of etiquette which is explained when you arrive. It was a traditional experience including a special dinner, sleeping on futons or tatami mats and enjoying the Japanese-style of public baths called *onsens*. These were where men and women were segregated and bathing naked, with a lot of etiquette surrounding the process. She added that in hotels and homes, she would find that bathtubs were short in length but very deep.

Samantha wanted to ask more about the Embassy and the people there, but her eyes had closed by then and she was suddenly woken up when Mary-Jo took her arm and said: "We are nearly there". Samantha could see that they were now in busy traffic in the city as Mary-Jo went on to tell her visitor that she would be staying in a very nice hotel for a few nights during her "settling in" period.

"And there is the Embassy", she pointed out at last, as they passed an elegant and tall modern building flying the Stars and Stripes over the entrance block. "This is the Akasaka district of the city and now you can see the Okura Tokyo hotel, it's just short walk away and you have a reservation there for your first week in Japan".

They pulled into the entrance of the stylishly elegant, 500-room hotel where Mary-Jo took Samantha to the reception desk and helped her through the necessary registration paperwork.

"You will be very comfortable here," said Mary-Jo as a porter bowed and took the luggage from the driver and picked up the electronic room key. "Have a good rest and enjoy the room service. There are good restaurants and also shops here for anything you might need. I will come to find you in the morning at about nine, if that is okay with you?"

"That sounds just fine and many thanks for looking after me… and for giving me such a full briefing on the way, so see you tomorrow" said a relieved Samantha as she followed the porter to the lifts, looking forward to a hot bath, a quiet evening and a good sleep before her first day at the Embassy.

CHAPTER 10
FIRST, DISCOVER JAPAN

There was tight security at the busy entrance to the American Embassy when Samantha arrived with Mary-Jo, as dozens more staff were also arriving at the start of their day. It was a large and imposing building and Samantha was taken through an impressively decorated lobby with a Stars and Stripes flag and a large, framed picture of the President. They took the lift to the second floor Intelligence section where Samantha was introduced to the CIA Station chief, Melanie Mackintosh, a small, alert-looking lady in her 40's with a firm handshake and a warm smile as she welcomed the new arrival. "Good to have you here for your first overseas posting, Sam," she began. "I've heard all about your work at Langley and it seems you have made a great start to a new career."

"Well thank you and thanks to Mary-Jo for looking after me so well," responded Samantha as she was offered a comfortable chair by a low table to be joined by the chief as a carafe of coffee arrived. When the two of them were left together, Melanie began to describe the organisation of the CIA team in Tokyo and described some examples of their work there, which included close liaison with the Japanese government's Public Security Intelligence Agency – "usually called the PSIA", she added, "And they are responsible for conducting surveillance of potential trouble-makers and all the usual intelligence-related work".

The chief went on: "I have to liaise with the PSIA on most of our activities here and they are pretty good people to work with, mostly bi-lingual and really efficient paperwork and records. You will see later that we have five other agents based in our team here and there is one empty desk in the ops room waiting for you – with nothing on it apart from our welcome pack – at least not yet! In the pack, you will find some maps of the area, information brochures, some tourist brochures and even a Japanese-English dictionary.

"But before you get involved in any operations", she continued, "I think it is important for all our new arrivals to discover more about Tokyo and the rest of the country and the ways in which everything seems different from any others. So I just want you to spend time familiarising yourself with the Japanese way of life as well as local geography and some of the history and traditions. In so many ways, it is very different from life back home."

"Yes, Mary-Jo gave me quite a briefing on our way from the airport yesterday as well" replied Samantha. "So I am beginning to understand what you mean".

Melanie continued: "So for the next couple of days, I suggest you get to know the guys here. Mary-Jo will take you to pick up your ID documents and a membership pass for the American Club from the admin office. And then, just start finding your way around this area of the city and then further afield. The others will give you some suggestions including the best ways for making some trips to the interesting places elsewhere in the country. In some cities, you should check in to the US consular offices to see what is going on - they are in Osaka, Nagoya, Sapporo, Fukuoka and Naha - you will see where these cities are in your information pack. And I suggest you use the trains where you can or rent a car – whatever you prefer."

She told Samantha that she was checked into the Okura hotel for a week and that she should then set off to see some other areas for the next couple of weeks – "You will get some advice from the others, but you will learn more by travelling on your own and when you come back, there will be an apartment ready for you nearby in a building belonging to the Embassy".

The briefing continued on the same relaxed lines, much to Samantha's relief and she began to believe that she would enjoy her time in Japan. She was reminded by Melanie not to be surprised to find that there were thousands of American citizens living in Japan, mainly military personnel and their families and also a large number of business visitors from the States, as well as tourists. So in the main cities, she would find English used a great deal and understood – but outside the business and tourism areas, people were predominantly speaking only the Japanese language and she should expect the same with road signs and other information.

Eventually, the chief stood up and said: "OK, Sam. I guess that's enough for now and it's time to introduce you to the rest of the team, or at least those who are here today and if there is anything else you need to know, just check with Mary-Jo in admin or come and ask me".

They walked out to the Ops area next door which immediately impressed Samantha. It was large and bright, with six semi-private open plan work-stations, each apparently equipped with two or three computer screens plus headsets, keyboards, phones and other office equipment, all neatly arranged across the desk area. She noted that there were two male operatives working busily in their units and one other unit occupied by a female agent. Two unoccupied units were strewn with documents and files but the sixth, as the chief had described, was ready and waiting.

"This is your base," she said. "So come and say hello to Bettina, Harrison and Jim – hi guys, this is Samantha who has just arrived from Langley to join us here."

"Just call me Sam," she said as she went to greet each of them as they walked from their desks to the centre of the room to meet her. "I know I have a lot to learn and I hope you will all help me."

"You bet," said an enthusiastic Harrison, who appeared to be about 30 and the youngest member of the team. And there were words of welcome from Bettina, a studious looking woman in her 40's and also from Jim, who was a rather older and dour-looking man – but no doubt with a wealth of experiences to pass on to a newcomer when he loosened up, thought Samantha.

"I will leave you to get to know these guys," said Melanie, walking to the door. "I've got work to do so I will see you later and good luck."

They all gathered round the table at the end of the room, which was equipped with a coffee machine and mugs. They each took a seat and relaxed, as Bettina poured them all coffee. Samantha had to remind herself that these three were all experienced CIA agents, especially when they asked her the usual "getting to know you" questions. But by now, she was becoming more confident in recalling her back story and was also able to describe her experiences during training in Virginia as well as her first two assignments, to Canada and Mexico.

"After all that, you will find it quiet here in Japan," said Jim, reassuringly. And Bettina added: "Maybe tomorrow I will take you to the American Club for lunch. You will feel at home there. But today let me walk you around the Embassy to get your bearings and then introduce you to the staff restaurant here for some lunch".

The four of them reconvened later to continue their convivial conversation over their lunch selections and then Samantha spent the afternoon becoming familiar with her work-station and the briefing information she found there – and also asking questions about the equipment around her. Jim showed her carefully how one screen was dedicated to the confidential link with the operations centre at the CIA headquarters in Virginia; another was set up to interrogate current information from the dedicated intelligence satellites covering the Pacific region; and the third was her computer for reading incoming documentation and messages and preparing her own reports and memoranda.

It was a full first day, she thought, as she strolled back in the cool Autumnal evening sunshine to the Okura Hotel for another opportunity to catch up with her jet lag.

CHAPTER 11

IT WAS NIKOLAI!

T he next day began with the regular departmental briefing from the Station chief on current operations and assignments – and there was another surprise for Samantha when Melanie referred to "the Ginza shooting incident" last week and related how two staff from the Russian embassy were still in hospital with gunshot wounds.

"This is being dealt with by the Tokyo police" she explained. "But because it involves a foreign embassy the PSIA people are also following up so we need to keep an eye on it." Melanie went on to ask her most experienced operative Jim to check on developments with his local contacts and to keep her informed. Then turning to Samantha she added: "This probably sounds like an everyday occurrence to you, Sam, with gun crime in the States at its present level. But here, shooting is almost unheard of. The gun laws are very strict and the bad guys seem to use knives, if anything."

Samantha had tried hard to show no reaction when the information about two injured staff from the Russian embassy was mentioned and she just nodded her understanding of the Station chief's report. She also began to think about how she could discover more details, since nothing further was added by Melanie. Who were the two Russians and what was their condition? And where could she find more information? This was still weighing on her mind as she tried to focus on studying all the documents and files she found waiting on her desk and it came as a welcome distraction when Bettina interrupted to suggest they should go to the American Club for lunch. First, they called into the admin office where Mary-Jo had her club membership card waiting. She also took the opportunity to tell Samantha that after checking out of her hotel on Saturday to set off on her travels, she could leave any of her luggage at the embassy until she returned when she would find it had been taken to the apartment assigned to her.

This was reassuring news for Samantha as they took the short taxi ride to the Club, which she discovered was a surprisingly spacious and bright, modern building with a range of facilities and with signs indicating at least three restaurants. There was a full-size swimming pool and a spa and also signs to the second-floor suites, presumably available for visitors. As she was being shown around, an impressed Samantha could see that the clientele using the Club facilities were from many nationalities and she wondered whether any of them were Russians? And then in the busy main lounge area she spotted a table with a selection of newspapers and magazines – including the New York Times and others in the English language. She hoped to find an opportunity to see if any of them had a report on the Russian shooting?

Bettina took her to the self-service restaurant and when they were seated with their choices, she began to outline some helpful suggestions for a sight-seeing period in Tokyo and around the country. Samantha tried hard to concentrate, but her mind was still on how to discover some local news about the Russian embassy victims without raising any suspicions.

As they walked back to the lounge after their lunch, Bettina was recognised by a couple who were just leaving and she told Samantha to go ahead and find some coffee for them both while she had a brief chat. This provided an opportunity for Samantha to quickly look at the range of newspapers, among them The Japan Times, which she was relieved to see was in English! She picked up a copy and took it to a corner table with their coffee and was starting to scan the headlines as Bettina arrived.

"This is interesting," said Samantha, quickly gathering her thoughts. "A Japanese newspaper in English. But like everything else here, I can see that the club really aims to make Americans feel at home."

Bettina agreed and explained that the Japan Times was a successful daily paper, mainly for the expats and tourists and that she would also find copies of most newspapers in the PR department at the embassy to stay in touch with events back in the USA as well as in Japan. She then said she needed to go to the reception desk to make some dinner reservations for the coming week, giving Samantha an opportunity to look more closely at the Japan Times. On page 3, she spotted a headline: ***"Two men in court for Ginza shooting"***. Reading on quickly, she focussed on the last paragraph:

"The incident occurred last week at the Nakai-Bar and left four people in hospital

with gunshot injuries including a diplomat from the Russian Embassy, Nikolai Aldanov, and Hideki Endo who is employed at the Embassy. Two other Tokyo residents were also injured in the incident, but their injuries are described as relatively minor and responding to treatment. Unconfirmed reports indicate that the Russian diplomat and his Japanese colleague are believed to have been the targets for the attack by the two accused, said to be members of the group protesting against the Russian occupation of the Northern Territories. They had apparently followed their victims from the Russian embassy to the crowded Ginza bar. Endo is still in intensive care at the hospital with serious chest injuries, but Aldanov and the other two men injured during the shooting, both Tokyo residents, are said to be recovering."

"Something told me that it would be Nikolai," Samantha thought to herself, but with a sense of relief that it could have been much worse news, and she was interrupted by Bettina who returned and said it was time to go back to the office…

During the afternoon, there were more briefings including instruction on the codes to use to activate her computer equipment and her sophisticated mobile phone which she was told was equipped with a GPS signal which enabled the embassy communications centre to track her movements. She was surprised that she actually found this reassuring, rather than intrusive.

As the CIA team was preparing to end their working day, Melanie returned to remind Samantha of their lunchtime conversation. "Go off for a couple of days to discover Tokyo and enjoy yourself," she said. "It will get you acclimatised and unless we contact you, don't come back to catch up here until Friday afternoon. So tomorrow, as I suggested, you could start with the Skytree."

At her hotel the next morning, the concierge told Samantha how to find the underground train to start her new experiences. At the Skytree station, she followed the crowd of tourists to the ticket windows before joining the line of many nationalities and voices. The lift to the top was an exhilarating ride and she could hardly believe the views across the enormous city of Tokyo and beyond, which were truly breathtaking.

"Now I feel I have really arrived in Japan", thought Samantha, as she read the information provided in several languages about the many landmarks she could see – and she also read that the Skytree had been opened in 2012, with the capacity in the upper conservatory for 900 people. Then she took her turn to climb the glass, spiral "skywalk" to the highest level with glass flooring providing a giddying view of the streets below.

In the distance, she could see the Japanese Imperial Palace and its gardens and decided that this should be her next stop. After another train ride, she discovered that the Palace was closed to visitors, but its Ninomaru Garden provided a welcome relaxing contrast to the crowded tower and the always-busy city streets. Then, following on from more of the advice from her office colleagues, she went to explore another aspect of Japanese life and history at the Sensoi Temple and then joined a small tour group to experience a Japanese Tea Ceremony.

As she had been told to expect in her earlier briefings, this required taking off her shoes at the entrance and wearing the slippers provided before crossing a wooden bridge and entering the traditional teahouse. Then there came the explanation of how to drink the Japanese green tea. This began by picking up the decorated handle-less cup with the right hand, ensuring that the decorative flowers are facing you. Next, she was told with an accompanying demonstration, how to support the cup with the left hand as you slowly drink the tea "in four sips".

During these familiarisation days, Samantha also tried Japanese restaurants, chatted to other tourists and used some useful words and phrases from her Japanese-English dictionary, and even found her way to the Ginza shopping area – with the opportunity for a quick look into the crowded and noisy Nakai Bar. "So this is where the shooting happened," she mused, and then thoughtfully strolled on her way for some window shopping.

She was becoming convinced that the recommended "CIA way" of finding her way around Tokyo alone was the best and fastest way to become acclimatized to her new environment – and not a reluctance from her colleagues to accompany her. But all these tourist distractions did not prevent Samantha from thinking about Nikolai in hospital and wondering how to find out more about his recovery. But there was nothing further in the newspapers that she could find.

When she returned to the Embassy on Friday afternoon, her office colleague Harrison invited Samantha to join him and his wife, Yua, for a welcome dinner that evening. But first there was a final briefing with Melanie, who provided some more advice on her itinerary for the next three weeks and reminded her about the areas where she was likely to find American military bases.

"I suggest you start with Hakone and see Mount Fuji close up", she advised. "And after that, you can head south and experience the famous bullet train from Tokyo to Osaka and don't miss having a day or two in Kyoto for some traditional Japanese history. And then try to leave yourself time to go to some of the Northerly areas before it starts getting cold there".

Samantha was bursting to ask questions but Melanie was clearly needing to deal with other business and reply to some waiting calls. As she wound up their session, she added: "You have a number to call me if you really need to, and we have your mobile phone number, but just enjoy yourself and get the feel of Japan. Finally, aim to get back here three weeks from Monday and you will be ready to move into your apartment and then get some action. So bon voyages…"

Back in the office, a somewhat bemused new arrival in the CIA team was relieved to find Harrison waiting for her with his Japanese wife Yua, who Samantha was delighted to see wearing a colourful kimono. She began to relax as they went by taxi to a traditional Japanese restaurant and her hosts introduced her to sushi, sashimi, tempora and yakitori as well as sake and amazake, all served decorously by quiet and calm waitresses, also in kimonos. This all ensured that she slept well and during the lengthy meal, she learned even more about life in Japan. Harrison carefully avoided talking "shop" which suited Samantha well as she relaxed at the end of a memorable first week in Japan.

Back at the hotel, she found a message waiting on her phone. It was from Tom Spencer at MI5 in London – he said that he was just checking that she had arrived safely in Tokyo and adding that she should call his direct line when she had an opportunity. She worked out that it would still be afternoon in the UK and decided to make the call.

He was warm and charming as usual and was pleased to know that her travel went as planned and that she was settling into her new surroundings. Then she quickly asked him if he had heard about the shooting incident in Tokyo and the condition of Nikolai Aldanov. He said he was 'in the picture" and asked her how much she knew?

"I saw in a local paper that he is recovering in hospital, but that his colleague is in intensive care," she said. "You will realise that I have to be very discrete here but perhaps you can find a way to discover the latest news and also whether he is going to stay here in Japan?"

"Yes, of course, Sam. We did pick up reports of the incident and you know that I fully understand your concern. It is always possible that he could still be useful to us one day and I will find a way to get you any news about him from our people at the Tokyo embassy," replied Tom. "So don't worry about it now and I think you should concentrate on your programme there."

"Well, it hasn't really started yet", Samantha answered. "They are insisting that I spend my first month here just getting acclimatised and travelling around the country".

"Good idea", said Tom. "Just enjoy it. I think they know that this will get you more familiar with everything and that you will then find it so much easier when you get your first assignments. There is a lot to learn about the geography of Japan and the way of life there. I have been there on several working trips and wish I could have spent longer, as you obviously will. So don't spend all your time at the American Club - and don't worry about you-know-who. I will keep a close eye on it and will find a way to let you know any developments. Safe travels."

And soon, it was Saturday morning and time for Samantha to pack her travel bag, check out from the luxury of the Okura Hotel and take her large travel cases to leave safely at the embassy before setting off into even more unknown territory on her somewhat daunting, unplanned tour.

CHAPTER 12
THE BULLET TRAIN

"Okay, I am on my own now so here goes," Samantha said to herself as she took the crowded subway to the even more crowded Tokyo Central station to start the next stages of her new adventure. Following the advice from her new colleague, Harrison, she decided to begin her tour with the closest of the places listed in her guidebook – Hakone. It was an 80-minutes train journey, much of it through the suburbs and industrial sites of the capital city, before reaching what were described as "the vast verdant forests" of the Hakone National Park.

At the station was a tourist office where a helpful bi-lingual man advised Samantha to take the Round Course ticket to see most of the highlights of the area in one day. This jncluded a visit to Lake Ashi and then a cable car ride followed by an unexpected and exciting walk on the Hakone Ropeway - "the longest suspension bridge in Japan? - to get a clear view of Japan's most famous feature, the snow-capped Mount Fuji.

This was a "wow moment" which Samantha could photograph and share with an equally impressed group of American tourists. Next, they went on to the Hakone Open Air Museum, an imaginative sculpture garden located on the mountain top with unusual sculptures which, as the guidebook accurately described, "integrated easily into the mountain landscape in their stunning design".

The tour continued its way back to the town of Hakone where Samantha decided it was time to check into what the guidebook recommended as a *Riokan* with a hot spring bath – and the Onsen Guest House seemed to match her objective of discovering more of the local experience. This involved the whole Japanese ritual of taking a long shower first, in order to enter the communal bath clean and scrubbed. She found the hot water was so relaxing and decided that it was no surprise that the Japanese had such a long life expectancy with such therapeutic and health benefits.

As she chatted to a Japanese couple with good English, they offered to guide her through a Japanese meal in the evening – fresh sushi, shrimp tempura, grilled Kobe beef, Yakatori, and more! And later, resting for the night on a low, Kumo bed, she could hardly believe the new life she was enjoying – and remembered that this was just a part of preparing her whatever may face her in the future as a CIA operative. She even asked herself whether she should be keeping her eyes open for suspicious-looking characters?

After more sight-seeing the next day, it was back to Tokyo to book her next experience, the Bullet Train to Kyoto. This famous high-speed train was so glossy and impressive, but even at a smooth 200 miles an hour, it took a while to leave the city behind. Samantha found herself yearning for the buildings to end but it seemed to sprawl endlessly until suddenly a passenger sitting on the other side of the train gesticulated as Mount Fuji appeared – again a truly majestic site, almost like it didn't belong - and despite the speed of the train, several minutes passed before it had been left behind.

Finally the countryside began, although she noted that the landscape was filled with paddy fields rather than cows or sheep. Many appeared to be small holdings, each being lovingly tended but then there were some bigger and probably commercial growing areas too as the train sped south.

Samantha knew from her guidebook that her next stop would take her into Japan's history in a city which was the country's capital until 1868. Kyoto, she read, had countless temples, shrines and other historical buildings. Her chosen target was Nijo Castle, built in 1603 as the Kyoto residence of the first shogun of the Edo Period. Then it became an imperial palace and it is described as the best surviving example of castle palace architecture of Japan's feudal era, and it was designated as a UNESCO world heritage site in 1994. She took her time among the slow-moving visitors to listen to the commentaries of the guides as they toured the entire castle and grounds, which are surrounded by stone walls and moats.

After soaking up her history lesson, she took a bus to the Biwako resort area just outside of Kyoto and travelled up to Mount Hiei on the Sakamoto cable railway, described as the longest cable car route in Japan! She had spotted that Mount Hiei is a world cultural heritage site as well as the birthplace of Japanese Buddhism. It also had fabulous views of Lake Biwa, the largest freshwater lake in Japan. She took photos and decided to stay at the Biwako Hotel, noting in her diary and the guest book that "the rooms are impeccable and the restaurant is amazing. Sorry to only stay one night".

The next target in Samantha's itinerary was Takayama and feeling bolder by now and with the help of the hotel concierge, she rented a car for a few days and found that her distant memories from England came back as she drove again on the left side of the road as she followed the GPS instructions for the three hour's drive. At this smaller town, she was delighted to find that she had chosen the right day. They were celebrating their annual festival with the people dressed in brightly coloured kimonos and incredible floats being paraded on the streets. Chatting to locals, she learned that during the rest of the year the floats are stored carefully in tall garages and that this was one of the two days of the year when they are brought out. This was another very different part of the country to experience, among the local people lining the streets to celebrate and watch the parades with many different national costumes, dances, music and traditions.

Again, she chose to stay in a local Riokan and after another hot spring bath she donned a traditional kimono and Japanese sandals found in her room and went out to find a restaurant for dinner. It was busy with happy Festival crowds, young and old, and she enjoyed mingling with them and listening to the excited chatter – and again, she paused to ask herself if this was really the new life of a CIA operative? And should she be using her training to keep her eyes open for the unexpected?

Most of the nearby eating places were full, but she found one with a friendly local lady to welcome her at the door who said sweetly in broken English that she could find a table for one. This time, she was faced with trying to decipher the menu in a town where nobody seemed to speak English. But with help from other customers and a patient waitress, she managed to avoid eating giblets or claws or something that she would not really fancy at all.

Next day, she decided that her trip to the southern part of Japan would not be complete without a trip to Nagasaki or Hiroshima – the only city names she recognised apart from Tokyo itself. So checking her road map, she decided to drive to Nagasaki, not knowing quite what to expect.

This led her to spend a somewhat disturbing afternoon in the Peace Museum, reliving the horrors of the atomic bomb which decimated the city at the end of World War Two and seeing pictures of the devastation it caused. She learned from the Museum information how Nagasaki was actually the second city to suffer the horrors of an atomic bomb. It explained how bad weather forced American planes to divert from their original target of Kitakyushu and bomb the city instead. She read to her horror that over 75,000 died and 75,000 were injured. To help her to appreciate the full scale of the destruction, she took the circular walkway leading down at the Museum, starting with attractive displays and photographic views of pre-war Nagasaki before the shock of entering a darkened room showing videos of the shattered city with stills of the dead and wounded. There was also a display of personal objects, including a schoolgirl's charred lunchbox and a helmet with the remains of a skull, to bring home the individual tragedy.

She then went on to see a smooth black stone column which marks the point where the bomb exploded some 500m above the ground. This had been the site of Urakami Cathedral, the largest Catholic Church in Asia, and where only a fragment of wall now remained. It all made her realise that if it were not for the memorials, the Museum and Peace Park, you'd never know that the quiet suburb of Urakami was completely destroyed.

In spite of the tragedy, Samantha could see that Nagasaki is now a beautiful city, with a huge bay and mountains framing the skies. It made her feel overwhelmed as she realised the resilience of the Japanese people to recover from such an experience. She also learned about the involvement of Winston Churchill and the US Presidents Roosevelt and Truman in the decision to use the ultimate weapon and this gave Samantha pause for thought about the history of recent international conflict – and she began to question the objectives of her own new career?

As she walked away, it was one of the few days on her travels when the heavens had opened and the wet weather seemed to fit in with her sombre mood. She soon found a café busy with tourists and after a glass of Japanese beer and a burger she was able to chat with a small group of Americans about the lessons they had all learned from their visit to Nagasaki.

She strolled thoughtfully in the light rainfall back to the modern Nagasaki hotel where she had found a comfortable room for her overnight stay, ready to make plans for the next few days. Although she had been checking her cell phone regularly, she was almost forgetting her briefing back in Tokyo until a bleep interrupted her bedtime preparations. It alerted her to a message: it instructed her to open the confidential line on the phone and key in the secret code she had been given. To her surprise, it worked first time and she found herself on the line to her office chief, Melanie.

"We know where you are," she began. "And you may not realise that we have been able to track all your movements. I'm glad you are getting to know the country and I am sorry to call you so late in the day – but I need to interrupt your plans. So could you get yourself to the American Consulate in Osaka tomorrow morning and meet up with one of our people there called Charles Madigan. He will brief you on a new assignment and then we will talk again – okay?"

"Yes, of course," replied Samantha, quickly adjusting to her business mode. "I have a rental car here and it looks like a couple of hours drive to Osaka so I will be on my way first thing. Anything else I should know or do?"

"No – just take it easy and get there safely," said Melanie. "We are really sorry to have to interrupt your travels and we know that you haven't been to Osaka yet. It's a really big city but your GPS will get you to the Consulate – we will talk again tomorrow. Sleep well."

CHAPTER 13

MORE HEADLINES

At GRU headquarters in Moscow, Yuri Bortsov was continuing to settle into his important new responsibilities as head of the 5th Directorate. He was given free rein to strengthen his team and reorganise procedures after the embarrassing Portsmouth incidents, as well as the routine business of setting up a series of new assignments for his top agents. The partial failure of the second Ricin attack in the UK had not created any negative problems, apart from concerns about the arrest of the two agents. "It will keep MI5 on the defensive and it showed the weakness of their security again" – that was the reassuring verdict he delivered to his senior bosses.

Bortsov continued to get interesting weekly reports from London on their monitoring of Tom Spencer's activities and also the Peters family, which helped him as he developed ideas for the next move. It seemed that all was going well… until the day when one of his assistants brought him a top secret file. He placed it carefully on the chief's desk and opened it to reveal a copy of a report in a British newspaper with the headline:

"MARINA PETERS: WHAT
REALLY HAPPENED?"

A shocked Bortsov could hardly believe what he was reading. An investigative reporter in London had reopened inquiries into the mystery surrounding "The Russian Lieutenant" and the funeral of Marina Peters.

It proved to be a lengthy and detailed review of all the events and developments following the Aldanov mission in the previous year. The reporter had been able to quote from new interviews with various people involved, including some of those who gave evidence at the trial of the Russian diplomat. Then at the end and in bold typeface, the article asked three questions:

"Was the Russian objective to silence the evidence against Aldanov?"

"Was the British secret service trying to discredit Russia?"

"Why are the official records of the events still being held in secret?"

At first, Bortsov was baffled by the tone of the report and asked his aide where it had come from and when it was published? He was told that it had arrived that morning from the embassy in London and had apparently been published in a Sunday newspaper just two days earlier. "Get me a call with the Ambassador," he demanded. "And get Dubinin to come up to my office at once."

The Directorate included a secret operation called "Section X", headed by an experienced technocrat, Mikhail Dubinin, which had the task of maintaining a register containing data on all the known agents working for the secret services of foreign governments around the world. And just ten minutes later, the head of "Section X" was already astonished as he read the article in his chief's office when the call to London came through.

"Have you seen the piece in the press about the Aldanov affair?" asked Bortsov. The Ambassador confirmed that he had read it and indeed he had asked for it to be sent immediately to Moscow. But he added that so far there had been no reactions in London, from the government or from the press.

"I don't really think there is anything new in the report," said the Ambassador, who went on to confirm that he would report immediately if there were any new developments.

Bortsov was feeling more suspicious as he ended his call to the London embassy. He turned to his section chief and asked: "Do you have anything further on this Marina Peters woman? As I read this new report in the press, I began to wonder yet again whether we had missed something important? Was she in fact working for British intelligence as a honeytrap and Aldanov fell for it? When I first read the background files, I was concerned about her Russian ancestry which must have made her an interesting prospect for MI5. Do some more digging with your people in London and see what else they can discover?"

There were the inevitable questions when a copy of the press report reached the Russian Defence Minister's desk later the same day and Bortsov provided some reassuring answers and confirmed that his team was following up urgently.

In the days that followed, the GRU agents in London were briefed to seek more background information about the Peters family. They discovered old photographs of Marina Peters and also talked to some of her friends and work colleagues. They eventually had a meeting with the reporter who wrote the new article, but they discovered nothing additional to the material in his report – except that a member of the British Parliament had been denied an opportunity to ask a question on the matter in the House of Commons.

CHAPTER 14
A DNA SURPRISE

Among all the other complex and secretive activities of the GRU each day, there were occasional communications with updates from the London Station chief on the contacts and inquiries being made by their agents, but no new developments. All information was analysed at regular review meetings… until the day came when an excited Dubinin asked for an urgent meeting with the General.

"I am not sure you are going to believe this," he began. "But in building up more information in our file on Marina Peters, we have been able to get background details on her early years and her jobs before she started to work for the British navy. Our guys in London did a thorough job as usual and they were eventually able to get access to her medical records. They even obtained her father's DNA by some subterfuge. I think they followed him to a café and then took his coffee cup. Okay so far?"

"Yes, go on," said an intrigued Bortsov.

"Well, quite separately from all this, it so happened that my team in Washington have been doing a routine update of their files on known American agents. This is a regular exercise, but in the course of their investigations they discovered the name of a new agent – she was the one involved in shutting down our cyber operation in Canada – I am sure you remember the case? Well, the woman from the CIA who worked on this is called Samantha Lord and they have been able to build up a profile from her stay in Canada. They even tracked her fingerprints and DNA from the hotel she stayed in – and guess what? The system has actually identified a match of her DNA with the data we have from Marina Peters' father. I found this very hard to believe and so I went through every detail with my experts and they say there is something like a 99.9% probability that this is the same woman – even though her appearance has been altered to avoid any photographic similarities."

Bortsov was silent for a minute as he absorbed this new information, shaking his head in disbelief. "That is an amazing piece of work," he said, and then added thoughtfully, "I am not quite sure what this means and I need to think more about it – but I knew there was something unexplained in that press story from London. So maybe the reporter was on to it, perhaps without even knowing the American angle?"

He started to read the file again and then asked: "So do you think that funeral in England could have been some sort of fake?"

"That's an interesting new line to follow up," commented an intrigued and eager Dubinin, already thinking he might have to make a personal trip to London on such a sensitive inquiry. Then his chief asked him: "Is it really possible to totally change someone's personality and appearance – but not their DNA? And how reliable is a father's DNA – and of course, he may not even be her biological father. Or maybe she had a sister or some other relative with matching DNA? What do you think?"

"Well, sir, I don't know what all this means yet, but it is remarkable discovery from the technical point of view," replied Dubinin. "Our system automatically cross-checks DNA data as a way of discovering possible relatives among the people in our records. But we have never found a match like this before. We are also going through another phase in our investigations by getting photographs of this Samantha Lord woman and then using computerised systems to compare her features with old photos of Marina Peters which our London guys discovered."

"Amazing – and apart from anything else," added the chief with growing confidence, "It also suggests that there are now more sophisticated ways to change an agent's appearance, that is apart from the DNA of course. This takes us a long way beyond growing facial hair and wearing a wig and spectacles, or even plastic surgery for the women. So why not get our guys in Tokyo to have a very discrete chat with Aldanov to see if he can recall anything else about his girl-friend and her family – I gather he is making a good recovery from that nasty shooting incident there by the way. But keep this DNA angle just between you and me for the time being.

"And can you start to track this new woman agent and find out what she is doing now, because if this is all true, then remember that if your news I correct, she also has a Russian family background, which could be useful. Let me think about all this and get back to you later. And well done to you and your team."

CHAPTER 15

A NEW CHALLENGE

T he main roads were very busy for Samantha's drive to the city of Osaka, wondering what had led to this change of plans? When she arrived at the American consulate, she found a car parking space for visitors and went inside to the reception area. Charlie Madigan, one of the locally-based CIA staff, came to meet her and he carefully checked her identity before leading her through the security system to a lift to the top floor. There in a small conference room, she was surprised to find that Melanie had arrived there from Tokyo to welcome her – and even more surprised to be taken next to the Consul's office where she was greeted by none other than Bob Smithers, the CIA boss from Langley HQ in Washington.

"Hi, you're looking great", he said as she walked into the room. "Sorry to interrupt your tour, but we have an important new assignment for you. Let's have a coffee and I will tell you and Melanie all about it."

When they were all seated and expectant, he began by explaining that the US Government has a secret programme which is managed by the CIA and the State Department called Armageddon. It was created to provide a central control system which would operate in the event of a major disruptive threat to the country such as a terrorist, nuclear or even a cyber attack. It consisted of several alternative underground locations around the world - including one in the Nevada desert, one in Canada and one in Europe - where the President or his designated advisers could be moved to enable the Government to continue to function.

And he added: "There is also one here in Japan, which is one of the reasons why the US maintains a strong military presence here".

The CIA chief went on to describe that these locations maintained 24-hour state-of-art readiness, supported by a flow of essential information which is fed by a pattern of secret codes distributed to them hourly by a military satellite system. However, they had recently suspected that these codes had been intercepted by Russia and suspicion had turned to Japan - either by Russians operating in the country or possibly there could be a spy among the military personnel manning the secret base… or a sophisticated combination of both. He added that their monitoring indicated that the confidential details were reaching Moscow about once a week over the past two months, usually at the weekend, so there was a regularity to be considered, among other things.

"And so, Samantha", he concluded, "Because of your Russian language experience in Canada and because you are also still unknown as a CIA agent, we are assigning you to try tracking down the leak. At the same time, we are following some other lines of inquiry, using Melanie's other agents on the ground here and other specialists from HQ who are tracking satellite data, and even drones to pick up coded signals – but we don't have a positive answer yet. So I guess you get the picture?"

This briefing brought Samantha back to earth with a bump after her relaxing travels and she quickly reassured Bob Smithers and Melanie that she now felt much more comfortable in the Japanese environment and was ready to get back to her first assignment – "It sounds like quite a challenge, but I understand what you are looking for," she added. "I guess the rogue American will be something of a needle in a haystack, but I guess there cannot be many of them with Russian contacts."

They went on to discuss a detailed plan of action and Bob revealed that their existing searches might have narrowed the location of the leak to a section in a military base on the island of Okinawa. He went on: "We have our biggest concentration of Defense Department resources there and it is a 2-hours flight south from Osaka. You will find it is quite a bit warmer than Tokyo so be prepared to travel like a tourist again, just like you did in Canada, and see if you can mingle in the right areas and find the American with Russian connections… yes, just like you did in Toronto," he repeated with a laugh.

"I don't think I can be that lucky again," replied Samantha, sharing the joke and as they relaxed, Melanie recalled some of the history of Okinawa and the Second World War battles in the Pacific region. She described how the American forces had fought there against some fierce Japanese defenders until the first atomic bomb was dropped on Hiroshima in 1945. "This decision meant that Japan surrendered and saved thousands of Americans whose lives would be lost if we had continued to invade the rest of the country to win the war," she added. "And I guess you saw something about this when you were in Nagasaki yesterday?"

Samantha had to remind herself that she was now an American – but without the background of an American education. She said she understood the argument raised by Melanie about lives saved by the horrific ending of the war which helped to put her visit to the Peace Museum into perspective. And she had learned enough on her travels to continue the conversation about her impressions of Nagasaki without questioning the moral issues it raised in her mind.

Bob Smithers said little about the subject but nodded understandingly and then told them: "Well, our job is to make sure we stay strong and avoid another conflict like that one. And I promise you that if things ever blow up again, it will be even worse with cyber wars threatening whole countries and their survival by attacking essential services like energy, transportation and telecommunications. This is why our new assignment here is so important. We just have to stay one step ahead and take counter-measures when there is a problem like this information leak to the Russians."

And turning to Samantha, he told her with a stern voice: "You are not alone, Sam. We are all doing the same job, even if you seem to be on a solo mission. So good luck and stay in touch with Melanie. I have to go now to see some other people with the Consul but I will be staying in Japan for about a week."

When the two women were alone, Melanie said: "Okay, Samantha, we need a night off. The office here has booked us into a nearby hotel so let's go to see some

Japanese acrobats and find some sushi. Forget work until tomorrow."

Over their hotel breakfast, Melanie resumed her briefing for Samantha's challenging assignment as a tourist in the island of Okinawa. Using a map, she explained exactly which of the many American bases there included the communications section and underlined one near the coastal town of Chatan which she described as a major hub.

She continued: "I have been in touch with my contact in PSIA, that's the Japanese security service, and they will check their records to see if any residents in the area are on their watch list and I will send you any new details. Also, I will give you the contact for our Company sleeper in the Okinawa capital, Naha – he is a long-retired American government man called Henry Gibson, married to a Japanese lady – so if you need any back-up or get into difficulty, contact him - and me, of course. And remember that we do not know the actual location of the Armageddon base. Apart from the military brasshats, no one here knows, except the Ambassador, and in fact, it may not even be here in Japan at all."

They went on to discuss how to get to the Osaka airport, where she would return her rental car, and then take one of the frequent flights for the two hours trip to Naha airport.

"Take care and good luck," said Melanie, as Samantha gathered her luggage and set off thoughtfully on another tourist trip – this time with another solo mission.

CHAPTER 16
AN UNFINISHED STORY?

At the MI5 headquarters on the banks of the River Thames in London, the Deputy Director Tom Spencer convened a meeting with his senior team and got their attention with his opening remarks:

"You all remember the Russian Lieutenant affair, I'm sure. Well, it seems that the Ruskis are sniffing around again – probably prompted by that piece in the Sunday Star last month about Marina Peters. We have a good idea who that journalist has been talking to, but he had nothing new in his story. So maybe they have been following the same trails in the hope of discovering something else. Any ideas?"

One woman officer suggested: "I am sure they will have targeted her father. They were a Russian immigrant family and he could still have useful connections for the GRU. In fact, they have probably had a trail on him ever since this business began."

"Well, he has been on our watch list all this time and there has been nothing suspicious," replied Tom. "But we have been more interested in his brother Andrew Peters, that's Marina uncle, who is more of an unknown quantity. Since he retired from the family business, he has been very active in local organisations in South London and seems to be close to some left-wing groups we have on our radar. So he is certainly one to keep an eye on and you may remember that he did ask some awkward questions about the cremation of Marina. I wonder if he said anything to the reporter to make him suspicious?"

Another of the experienced MI5 officers, John McDonald, reminded the group that had been a BBC journalist in his early career and he said: "Let me start by talking to the reporter at the Sunday Star – his name is Roger Stanton and I may have met him somewhere in earlier years. I will see how much he knows?"

Tom Spencer agreed and went on to assign other members of his team to pick up the trail of the agents from the Russian Embassy who had been tracked on a visit to Portsmouth in the previous week. "Find out where they went, who they spoke to and what they might have discovered. I will deal with the Navy brass myself through the MOD security people – so keep me in the picture on a daily basis."

John McDonald had stayed in touch with several of his media contacts, who had often proved useful in his second career. These did not include Roger Stanton, but he knew just the man to use as a discrete go-between – a BBC security correspondent who he knew had followed up on the Sunday Star re-hash of the Marina Peters story. Between them, they set up an opportunity to meet in the comfortable lounge of a large London hotel in the early evening.

As planned, when John arrived he found his BBC contact and Roger Stanton relaxing in plush armchairs and chatting over their drinks. He was introduced as an old friend as he joined them, but when the waiter came to take their order for drinks the BBC man said he had to leave for another appointment.

"I am sure you are not here to talk about the weather," said Roger as they settled down with their choices of whisky. "In fact, I have been expecting a contact from MI5 since I wrote my piece about that Russian Lieutenant and the woman from the Navy. My guess is that this is it, right?"

"Yes, and I know you understand that we had to find the right time and to do it in confidence," said John in a warm and friendly tone. "That was an interesting piece of work you did, but we have been wondering why you decided to follow up the story now? I don't think you told us anything new."

"Well, we heard a few rumours from Portsmouth that the Russian Embassy and you guys were still keeping an eye on the various people involved," Roger replied. "And when I started to follow up with some inquiries, I found that there were still doubts in some people's minds about what really happened – and that was the headline, as you know."

John encouraged the reporter to talk through his recollections of the interviews with Marina Peters' family in London, and her friends and neighbours in Portsmouth. He described how the police and navy people were "more than usually tight-lipped" when he contacted them – which had intrigued him. Some of the friends and former colleagues of Marina had told him how they had received calls and visits from strangers asking about Marina – they were foreigners and were assumed to be Russians. He then recalled that one of her closest friends told him that an unknown caller had even asked if she knew the names of Marina's doctor and dentist.

They chatted for more than half an hour and John was satisfied that the reporter had no new facts to work on but would probably continue to regard it as a good unfinished story. And Roger decided that this unexpected follow up by MI5 confirmed that there might be more to come. But as they parted, Roger was happy to agree that their meeting had "never happened".

As John McDonald and other members of his team reported back in the following days, Tom Spencer found that those who had been involved in the Royal Navy command in Portsmouth and at the Ministry of Defence regarded the whole matter as "case closed". But he became increasingly concerned about the new Russian interest – and particularly the casual reference to "doctors and dentists" passed on by the Sunday Star reporter. His past experiences told him that this could only mean that there was a question about identity in their new investigations. But why could that be relevant when the series of events in Portsmouth had ended with a cremation?

Had the Russians actually succeeded in rumbling his clever plan in some way? And if they had, what could they gain from it? He had succeeded in getting one Russian agent sacked and their London spymaster jailed. He had also saved the life of a very bright woman and helped to create a new CIA operative. From his perspective, it was still Britain three and Russia nil!

CHAPTER 17

WHERE TO START?

At Naha airport, Samantha rented a small car and used her GPS directions to head for the small town of Chatan, shown in her tourist map as the closest place to the American base identified for her during her briefing in Osaka. Her research during the previous evening had told her that it was also a coastal resort with a Hilton hotel, so she had prebooked a room for a week.

On the way, her route by-passed Naha city and she appreciated that Okinawa was an attractive island with open countryside and distant mountains as well as some interesting features she had read about in her tour guide. If she had the time, she knew there were restored castles to visit, white sandy beaches and clear blue seas with coral reefs and whale watching. It was hard to remind herself about the tragic losses suffered in this same island by the Japanese and American forces in 1945.

After about an hour's drive, there was another reminder when she saw the signboards and buildings indicating that the US Army was there, in large numbers. Before she arrived at the hotel in Chatan, she passed some of the older and traditional Japanese homes and then to her surprise, there was a modern shopping mall which looked as though it had been transferred from the suburbs of Washington DC. She decided it was going to be a strange combination of Japan and America as she set about her challenging task.

The hotel was what she expected – a smart and efficient Hilton, but with mostly Japanese staff. At the door, a uniformed valet bowed and took her car keys to park in the hotel garage. A porter took her luggage and escorted her to the check-in desk where the clerk was polite and charming and spoke perfect English. Her room was spacious and bright, with a distant sea view, and there was an American channel on the TV. As she unpacked her bags, Samantha said to herself: "This will be perfect for a week, or maybe more… but this time I have work to do."

But where to start. That was the problem.

She found a text message on her phone from Melanie with the contact name and phone number of the CIA's local 'sleeper'. Then she went out to begin with a stroll around the neighbourhood which was an interesting mixture of traditional Japanese shops and restaurants, new apartments and the shopping mall, with a combination of familiar store names and local companies. Most of the shoppers appeared to be Japanese residents or possibly tourists but there were also groups of American women who she assumed were military wives. She recalled her mission to Canada where it had been more difficult to identify which were the Russians among the local population until she discovered their national restaurants. Now, she thought, she would have to find a way to meet up with

Americans and maybe gossip among the wives might be a way to get a sense of who does what and where?

She stopped by at a coffee shop, choosing one which was busy so that she would have to share a table after collecting her cappuccino. She politely interrupted the conversation among three women who seemed delighted to say 'hi' to someone new. "Where are you from?" asked one.

"I have just arrived from DC a month ago to start a job in Tokyo," Samantha explained. "But I am trying to see as much of Japan as I can before I get too busy and Okinawa was one of the places I was advised to see while I had the time. So I just flew in today from Osaka."

"So what do you do?" came the quick and typically direct American question.

"I work for the Government," she replied. "So I am based at the embassy in Tokyo for a year or so and I am lucky to get to such an interesting country. How do you get on with the language?"

The three women laughed and one said: "We don't bother with it much. There are so many of us here that it is much like being posted to Texas."

"So what do you all do here to fill the time?" Samantha asked.

"Have fun" they all agreed, and they went on to describe in detail the local activities which they enjoyed including the American club with its swimming pool and gymnasium, the golf courses and tennis courts, visiting each other for coffee mornings and playing bridge. Then there is the beach and sailing boats. "How's that for starters," said the main spokesperson for the group. "And the weather is just like California, so what is there not to like?"

"How about your menfolk – I guess you are here with military husbands?", said Samantha.

"Sure thing, when we see them," came the reply. "They keep pretty busy on the base but they seem to like the assignment here and we all have a good social life at the weekends. Joanne here has a man with a nice boat which is great for parties… and sometimes for a trip around the other parts of the island. It is real pretty in places."

"That's what I want to see, as well as some of the local history," commented Samantha and turning to the lady on her right, she added: "Hello, so you are Joanne, I'm Samantha but everyone calls me Sam". The others then introduced themselves as Kim and Donna as they all relaxed and ordered another coffee. They went on to chat about shopping and their families and Samantha explained that she was single and a career girl, but before getting any more questions, she decided it was time to move on.

"It's been so good to meet you so soon after arriving here," she said. "It's been a lovely chat. I am close by at the Hilton for a few days so why not stop by at the bar one evening and I can discover lots more about life in Okinawa. Bi for now."

And she left, her new friends exchanged their reactions to meeting this woman from the Government – "likeable but a bit mysterious" was their verdict, but they were sufficiently intrigued to consider a follow up meeting at the Hilton one day.

Samantha returned to her room, pleased with the success of her first attempt at making a contact with the Americans in Chatan, and after changing for the evening, she decided to try the hotel bar before going to the restaurant for dinner. It was quite busy, mostly American men it seemed, and she attracted a few eyes as she found a gap to reach the bar and order a Campari and soda. "Hi ma'am, that's a pretty drink," ventured the nearest of the men. "You a new arrival here?"

"Yes, flew in today – just on a sight-seeing tour", replied Samantha. "Seems like I am back in America at the moment."

"Yep, not many locals in these parts, but I guess you will feel at home here. Where are you from?"

"Washington, DC, but I've just started a new job in Tokyo and I have some time off to see the best parts of Japan," she replied. "I liked the sound of Okinawa and Chatan but I didn't expect it to be full of Americans. It seems like I've found an Army town here."

"That's right – and air force too like me," he continued. "I'm Gus, by the way. It's a pretty good posting for us. Just showing the flag and making sure the Japs stay on our side. But we don't see much of them here. It's probably a bit different in Tokyo, I suppose. Never been there, but maybe I will one day."

"Well, I'm Sam, short for Samantha, and I hope you make it to Tokyo," she replied with a cheerful smile. "It's a great city and so different to anywhere else I have ever been, but I am trying to see as much of Japan as I can while I have the opportunity."

Gus turned back to his group of pals as told them: "Hey guys, this is Sam. She's from DC and touring the country, so say hello and welcome. They turned to look, waved a hand and returned to their pints of beer. So Gus continued: "They are a bit shy, we don't see many strangers here. Come and join us?"

Samantha thanked him warmly and explained that as she had flown in that day, she planned to have an early meal and then a good night's sleep before setting off to see more of the island the next day. She was assured that Gus and his group were in the Hilton bar most evenings and he said they would keep an eye open for her.

And so it was a quiet evening with a very American room service meal of Caesar salad and a slice of cheesecake to end a what Samantha regarded as a good start to her new assignment. She fell asleep thinking about how to widen these early contacts with the military – but also remembering that in her training programme back in Langley, one of the psychologists had said that a characteristic of a typical informer or spy was being a 'loner' and an introvert. She clearly had a long way to go…

CHAPTER 18
SEEKING A "LONER"

A fter an early hotel breakfast, Samantha decided to explore more of Chatan and began with a long walk along the seafront area. She found herself studying the joggers, men and women, taking their morning exercise in the cool sunshine. Some were Japanese, but most of them appeared to be Americans – and perhaps these were the 'loners'? This might be a long search, she decided, but on her way back to the hotel she stopped at the shopping centre to find a pair of jogging shoes, a tee-shirt and a suitable light-weight track-suit – things she had not thought of packing for her travels.

Back in the hotel reception, she asked the parking attendant to collect her car and while waiting she chatted to the concierge about some of the nearby historic areas. In perfect English, he described two locations which were just a few miles away and, in her brochure, he highlighted Nagagusuku Castle and the Futen Manzan Jinguji Temple and gave her the driving directions.

She was not disappointed by his advice. She discovered that the castle, now in ruins, was wonderfully picturesque. She joined a group of mostly Japanese tourists as a guide explained in both languages that it was one of a number of castles built on the island of Okinawa by the Ryukyu Kingdom in the 15th century. It was a fortress built to defend the region against attacks from the east. The tour guide told the Americans in her group how the castle was visited in 1853 by Commodore Matthew C. Perry who had sailed his fleet across the Pacific and is credited with opening up trade and exchanges between Japan and the rest of the world after 200 years of isolation. In his report, he noted that the walls seemed to be designed to absorb cannon fire since the six courtyards of the fortress had "stacked stone walls". The castle, or gusuku in Japanese, was added to the list of UNESCO World Heritage Sites in 2000.

As Samantha chatted with some fellow Americans in the tour group, they all decided that this was not only an interesting visit but also a useful subject for future conversations. None of them had previously heard about Commodore Perry. "He was not in our history lessons", said one.

Next, after stopping at a convenient MacDonalds on the way, it was on to Futen Manzan Jinguji Temple, and in the car park she saw a tour bus unloading the same group she had accompanied at the castle. Some of the Americans greeted Samantha like a friend as they were all welcomed with a polite bow at the entrance by another bi-lingual guide for a very different tour. This was a traditional religious experience at a typical Japanese temple and shrine. The temple belonged to the Toji Shingon Shu sect of Buddhism and contained a shrine built in 1459 on the orders of the king of Ryukyu, the central region of Okinawa.

"So, we have had quite a baptism of Japanese history and religion today", said one of the Americans to Samantha as they left. "Where are you from?"

As they walked to the adjoining tea shop, Samantha explained that she was now working in Tokyo but was taking some time to explore more of the country. They were an older group of retired Americans and in the relaxed conversation, she mentioned casually that she was working at the Embassy in Tokyo – and was taken by surprise when one man in the group said: "Ah well, I may see you there. I have an appointment with the Ambassador when we get back there next week. I expect you know Patrick Sullivan? He is an old business friend of mine."

Samantha was taken aback and realised that she could not even remember the name of the Ambassador and had certainly not met him. She quickly covered her tracks by explaining that she had joined the Embassy staff only a couple of weeks earlier and had been told to go away and travel for a few weeks to acclimatise to the Japanese way of life, so had not yet had time to meet the Ambassador. "Yes, that's typical of Patrick," said the stranger. "He's a thoughtful man - starting you off with some travels to get the lie of the land. I will tell him we met in Okinawa – what's your name?"

He wrote her name in his pocket diary and Samantha asked the couple where they were from. They continued with a more relaxed conversation about New York City and he was happy to talk about his experiences in the financial business until it was time for the bus party to leave.

Samantha realised that she had probably said too much to a stranger as she took a circuitous route around the southern part of the island, enjoying the views and the colourful local villages. On the way back to the Hilton, she decided to visit the bar again in the evening. She found that Gus was there, this time sitting at a table with a man and two ladies – and a bottle of white wine. He saw her arrive and invited her to join them where he introduced his wife, Mandy, and the other couple as Hal and Rose, who was Japanese.

"Good to meet you," said Mandy. "Gus told me about you and said it was interesting to meet a visitor from the States who is not from the military. Have you been sight-seeing today."

Gus pulled up another chair, poured Samantha a glass of wine, and she started to describe her visits to the castle and the temple. The two ladies had obviously not taken the opportunity to see much of Okinawa beyond Chatan and even asked if she "felt safe"? Gus went on to explain how there was a great deal of resentment among locals about the American presence on the island, with over 20,000 troops and about 23 military bases. "It's not so much the hangover from the war itself," he explained. "But the US Government took over Okinawa in 1945 and did not hand it back to Japan until 25 years later. So there is a long history of anti-American feelings and some of the Japanese restaurants around here do not welcome Americans. So we all like to get here to the Hilton and we are planning to get a T-bone steak tonight. Would you like to join is?"

Samantha showed some polite reluctance to intrude on their evening, but then agreed because she realised that it was another opportunity to learn more about the US operations. She declined the suggestion of a Texas-sized steak and enjoyed a chicken Caesar salad as the wine relaxed them and the conversation ranged over their family stories and eventually to their jobs on the base. Gus was a pilot, frustrated by failing to make the grade as an astronaut and now flying supply planes. Hal was more reticent, but encouraged by Rose, he said he was a cyber communications expert. She added, proudly in her broken English: "He doesn't say much about it because nobody understands what he does."

Reflecting on her day as she prepared for bed, Samantha was pleased that she had now confirmed the presence of cyber communications activity at the Chatan base. Her decision to start her inquiries in this location and at the Hilton had probably been the right one.

The next morning it was time to try her newly acquired sporting outfit and join the joggers on the waterfront before breakfast. She found a steady flow of solo runners, only a few of whom appeared to be locals. They were mostly men – but with a few women running in pairs. At the southern end of the esplanade she could see some of them entering or leaving the guarded gates of the military base. Beyond were various red brick buildings and then a group of at least six satellite dishes of varying sizes and two tall telecommunications towers, which also confirmed that she was in the right place for her mission. Even further away, she could hear and occasionally see aircraft landing and taking off in what was clearly a busy military and air force complex.

She kept moving with the flow of runners as she took in these important sightings – but she was not as fit and fast as most of them and after a further half a mile or so, she was pleased to discover a refreshments kiosk with a few seats and a friendly Japanese man serving juices and chilled water. "Hi madam", he said with a small bow. "You new here?"

Samantha took a bottle of sparkling water and as he continued to serve other runners, she explained that she was on vacation and worked in Tokyo. "Aha, not army then. Nice to see you here to enjoy our sunny island," he said. Another female runner, about the same age as Samantha, overheard this and sat down with her orange juice to join in. She was inquisitive about the choice of Okinawa for a vacation, but when she heard about the other places Samantha had visited in the previous week, she said she understood and wished she had time to see much more of Japan. She continued to ask about Samantha's work in Tokyo and before that in Washington. When Samantha tried to change the subject by saying: "I had no idea we had so much military here", the woman commented that this surprised her for someone working in the US Government and went on to press her further on her past experiences.

"I'm just an administrator, a paper pusher," Samantha explained. "And I have only just arrived in Japan. My boss said that newcomers are much more useful if they start by getting a good understanding of Japan's geography and customs and they sent me off for a couple of weeks – she called it acclimatisation."

"Very nice, too – and I am Georgina, by the way" she replied, and Samantha returned the compliment, becoming more curious about this quite sophisticated woman. She learned a few more things about women in the military and eventually, she was emboldened to ask: "So what exactly do you do?"

"If I told you, I'd have to shoot you," she replied. They both laughed as they moved away to continue their exercise jogging and she added with a wave: "Hope to see you again one morning."

CHAPTER 19

WHO IS THIS WOMAN?

At "The Diamond" in Moscow, the mysterious discovery about Marina Peters and her DNA preoccupied Yuri Bortsov and he decided to share the information with his boss at the Ministry. After hearing the details, the Minister agreed that the sensitivity of this new development made it essential that there should be no leak at this stage. "Also try to get on the tail of this new agent our people found in Canada and find out how the CIA are using her," he said. "Her assignments could reveal whether she has the same Russian background as the Peters woman."

Bortsov confirmed that this was exactly what his team was working on and said he would report back with any new developments.

The digital communications group in Mikhail Dubinin's section had used a range of information sources and digital tracking tools to build up their records on hundreds of CIA operatives and informers. In many cases, this work enabled them to track their locations and movements with a high percentage of accuracy. However, frequent changes of codes and passwords often frustrated their efforts to read messages – but, as instructed, they had eventually succeeded in tracing the existence of Samantha Lord, starting with her operation in Toronto which was linked to the unexpected raid on the agency's cyber operation in the city.

In one of his regular meetings with Bortsov, Dubinin said he could report limited success. They had been able to track her to a recent flight from Washington DC to London – but after that, her movements had 'gone cold'. She did not appear to be using the usual telecommunications links back to CIA headquarters – but their UK-based agents were continuing to monitor all possible channels in their efforts to locate her. He also added that she had talked to one of their contacts when she was in Canada, but he had reported that she did not appear to speak or understand Russian. This seemed to match the information from London that although Marina Peters' family came from Russia, she had been born and educated in Britain and that she would not have been employed by the British navy if there had been any question concerning her loyalties.

"If all that is true," Bortsov, asked Dubinin, "And just supposing for a moment that these two women are actually one and the same person, then she could be in London to see her old friends and family again. Are you checking that? And if she does not have any current Russian connections, why did the CIA go to so much trouble to give her a new identity? What is actually happening now with that reporter in Portsmouth?"

"Maybe it was just some sort of experiment?" replied the cryptology and cyber communications specialist. "That reporter interviewed most of the people originally involved and our agents have followed up with all of them in the past couple of weeks, including the Peters family. But there is nothing new to work on except that the navy and Government people are still refusing to say anything, which is a bit suspicious a couple of years after what happened."

Bortsov then suggested another line of investigation. "What exactly happened with that second operation in Portmouth dockyard? We know that the man from MI5 who knew all about the Peters and Aldanov story got away unscathed and that it was one of his staff members, another woman, who was the victim. Take another look at that incident. Who else was there? It must all be linked in some way and the MI5 man is at the centre of it. Find out what happened to that woman as well and how they are linked together?"

"Yes, good idea," replied Dubinin. "I will look into that. But meanwhile, we know that this new agent is somewhere out there doing the CIA's work, probably travelling as a tourist. And yes, we will have our London people keep a close eye on the Peters family and the team working with Spencer, that's the MI5 man you mentioned. But I believe that whoever this woman is, she is certain to surface and make contact eventually and we will find her."

CHAPTER 20
A HELPFUL JOGGER?

During another day of sight-seeing around the island in her small rental car, the brief conversation with Georgina, the jogger from the military base, was on Samantha's mind. Was this a useful contact she could follow up – perhaps more easily than trying to get closer to the men she met in the hotel bar? The size and importance of Okinawa to the US military was confirmed to her as she drove past one establishment after another, and she felt that seeking one rogue informer among such a huge number of service personnel and their families might be an impossible task. There was also the possibility that the bases employed local people to provide support services – although on second thoughts she realised that this would be unlikely in areas handling secret information. The daunting task was like looking for a needle in an enormous haystack, but she did not want to ask Melanie for any help or support just yet.

Back in the hotel bar that evening, some members of the same group were there and although there was no sign of Gus, she had a cheery welcome from Hal who appeared to be on his own at the bar. "Hi Sam", he called across the busy room. "Care to join me for your Campari this evening?"

She was surprised at first and as she went to the bar stool next to him, she recalled that Hal had been the quiet one on the previous evening, disclosing only that he worked in the cyber communications area at the base. He continued to say little, but he was friendly and asked about her travels that day and where she was planning to go next. He also became inquisitive about her current job and previous career and Samantha soon realised that he was a very intelligent and studious man who was actually weighing her up carefully – even suspiciously. She changed the subject by asking about Rose, but he quickly explained her absence at a badminton club and returned to try some more searching questions. Samantha was relieved when two of his colleagues arrived to join them and he introduced her as "Sam, the mystery lady from Tokyo."

When the others reacted to this description, Hal added: "I think Sam is more important than she lets on because they have given her three weeks to get to know Japan before she starts her new job at the Tokyo embassy. That's right, isn't it Sam?"

"Well yes," she replied, adding as modestly as she could: "Well, all I can say is I am lucky to have got this assignment because I have never travelled to the Far East before and my boss said I have lots to learn before I can be of much use at the Embassy. So do you guys work with Hal?"

"Sure do," said one. "He's our boss and he doesn't give us three weeks off for anything."

They all continued to chat about their limited knowledge of Japan until Samantha decided it was a good moment to leave them, but wondering whether and how to try to pursue the contact with Hal again? She decided to order room service and have an early night to consider her options. She felt she had made some progress on her own but what was the next move? Who would be the best prospect to pursue further – was it to be Hal or should she try to follow up first with Georgina?

She slept well and decided to start the day with the jogging group again. After a while, as she had hoped, she spotted Georgina who was on her own and coming from the direction of the military base. Her greeting was reciprocated and they continued to run gently together for ten minutes or so until eventually arriving at the refreshments café. "You are much fitter than I am," said Samantha breathlessly as they lined up at the counter for their cooling juices. Her new friend just laughed and said she should "keep it up" as they sat down together.

"It was nice to meet someone new who is not from the base," said Georgina, cheerfully. "I wondered whether I would see you here again and here we are. So when are you moving on to continue your tour?"

"Not for a few days," replied Samantha, who lowered her voice to ask: "I must say I was intrigued by your reply yesterday about your job at the base. I take it that you are doing something hush-hush, and as it happens, I am not actually on vacation here. I am doing some research here for an American business and I would quite like your advice? Can we chat again somewhere quieter in the next day or two?"

"Okay. I understand and that sounds like a good idea," said Georgina, looking around cautiously at those who were chatting with their refreshments at nearby tables. "It would be nice to get to know each other better so maybe we could meet up somewhere quiet for a meal. How about this evening?"

She wrote down the address of a Japanese restaurant and handed it to Samantha. "Shall we say about 6.30?" she asked, adding: "And by the way, I am Georgina Winters, First Lieutenant, Army Intelligence Group 4, if you need to check me out". Samantha reciprocated with her surname, and the evening rendezvous was agreed as they went their separate ways among the other joggers.

CHAPTER 21
FINDING A SUSPECT?

A part from a stroll around the town for a lunchtime sandwich and checking out the location of the Hama Sushi restaurant she had saved on her notepad, Samantha spent much of the day at the hotel writing up notes on her contacts and considering her next moves. When should she 'break silence' and report back to her boss in Tokyo? She realised that they would know from their tracking system that she was still in Okinawa and would also know it would be a long and slow task to try to locate the source of the problem. However, she had discovered an interesting contact in the military and before going any further, it would probably be prudent to check on Georgina's credentials.

So she decided to send a confidential message to Melanie asking her to make a security check on First Lieutenant Georgina Winters from Army Intelligence Group 4 based in Chatan, Okinawa, as a possible "useful contact." Within 30 minutes, Melanie was on her secure phone line:

"Good to hear from you," she began. "This sounds like an interesting contact. We have run a check and I can tell you that Lieutenant Winters is confirmed by the Department of Defense as an experienced officer with top security clearance. So what are you planning?"

Samantha explained how she had met her contact and discovered that she might have some connection with the communications department staff at the military base. "I have planned to meet her for dinner this evening and it might turn out to be a non-event – but it seemed worth following up if she is reliable. I may have to tell her about our objectives if things go well."

"Take it one step at a time, Sam," said Melanie. "But I am sure you know how to handle this and good luck. Let's have an update tomorrow."

As she entered the restaurant promptly at 6.30, Samantha could see that this was an elegant and traditional meeting place and Georgina was already there, seated cross-legged at one of the large low tables decorated with oriental flower arrangements. One of the serene, kimono-clad staff escorted her to join her new friend and to present them both with a glass of sake. "This is a wonderful place, obviously very special," Samantha said, as they raised their glasses for the first sip.

She took a few minutes to find a comfortable low level position and after they had chatted for a few minutes about the restaurant and Georgina's previous experiences there, the first courses of food arrived. There was obviously no requirement to study a menu or place an order – everything had been arranged. So the sake was regularly replenished as they worked their way slowly through the succession of dishes, from sashimi and tempura to the shabu-shabu hot pot.

As they relaxed and got to know each other better by the minute, they swapped stories about their respective careers, which Samantha handled very carefully and went on to compare their experiences with the lives of the military wives she had met during her evenings at the Hilton Hotel. "They were so boring," she said. "They had not even bothered to see more of Japan but just kept themselves together in a sort of cocooned world."

"I know, because I tried it when I was much younger", agreed Georgina, who went on to explain that she was brought up in an army family and lived near a large military base in California. Not surprisingly, like many of her friends, she had married a handsome soldier when she was 22 but discovered within a couple of years that his whole life was taken up by his army friends, his army duties and every kind of sports activity. She added wistfully: "And he was not even the slightest bit ambitious and we were going nowhere. But there were new opportunities coming up at that time for women in the services, so we soon drifted apart and went our separate ways. Although I was already four years out of college, I applied for an army scholarship and was accepted. And then, after a lot of training and hard work, I became a junior officer and was assigned to military intelligence".

"That's so impressive," replied Samantha. And with that, and as the table was cleared to make way for a large dish of assorted fruit, she decided to tell her new friend more about her reasons for being in Okinawa: "Actually I work for the CIA and I have come here on a special mission."

"Hmmm – do you know, Sam, I rather suspected that from your demeanour yesterday", came the calm reply. "So I am not surprised. And yes, we are both involved in confidential stuff. I actually work in military intelligence, so I come in touch with some of your people occasionally. But I have not met those based in Tokyo yet because I have only been assigned here for a couple of months and still have a lot to learn".

Samantha decided to explain that she had been an agent for less than a year, after doing all the training courses at Langley in Virginia and that so far she had been assigned to carry out solo missions in Mexico and Canada. After she had described them in some detail, Georgina said she was impressed and added that when she completed her ten years in the military, she would be really interested in a second career with the CIA. Then coming to the point, she asked: "So how can I help you?"

"It's like this," said Samantha. "Our cyber experts in Langley have discovered that the Russians have got hold of some of the codes to access international transmissions. Apparently, the codes are changed daily and somehow, they have traced the leak of these changes to Japan. Then they narrowed it down to Okinawa and it seems that your operation here is the telecoms hub. So my simple – ha ha - job is to nose around here to see if anyone knows the culprit. How does that sound?"

"Yes, real cloak and dagger stuff – and I don't envy you that one," came the first reaction. "But actually, there are very few people in the comms centre who would be cleared to know this sort of information or who could pass on the details of how to intercept it. And they would all have top grade security clearance with regular oversight measures. I think we can trust each other, so can you tell me any more, like dates and times so that I can find out who was on duty?"

"Not exactly, but we believe this is a continuing problem, not just a one off," said Samantha. "The existence of the secret information appearing in Russian hands has been detected as a weekly occurrence over the past couple of months, apparently at the weekends. So I think it really comes down to discovering whether there is anyone suspicious at the base there, perhaps with a Russian contact?"

Georgina began by describing how her job included monitoring the activities and records of those in the communications section with security clearance. There were three teams, she said, each made up of four highly qualified operators working in shifts, 24 hours a day and seven days a week. There were also three officers involved in managing the section. Her job included maintaining their records, reviewing their backgrounds, screening their personal activities and contacts, and checking for any health issues or concerns.

This seemed to confirm to Samantha that this was a promising contact, so she did not pursue it further as they decided to have one final drink before calling it a day and telling her new friend: "I am so glad we met and many thanks for listening to all the details of my task here. Give me a call if you have any further information. I will be staying around the hotel tomorrow……"

CHAPTER 22

CHECKING ON ALDANOV

It was the next day when Dubrinin rushed upstairs at the GRU headquarters in Moscow and breathlessly told his boss: "I think we have found the woman and she is in Japan. And we also discovered that the CIA Deputy Director from Langley, a man called Smithers, flew to Japan a couple of days ago and we know that he was the mastermind behind Samantha Lord's recruitment as an agent. And what is more, we think we have tracked one of her messages which has been located to Osaka and one of our guys there is on the trail."

"Good work again," said Bortsov. "But what is going on in Japan? Things have been pretty quiet there lately so I will have a word with our ambassador in Tokyo next and see what he knows?"

It was still early evening in Japan, so he immediately booked a hot-line call to General Malinov and they renewed their previous experiences together in the defence ministry before he started outlining the story so far and asked: "Is anything happening there which would bring the top brass from the CIA on a visit to Tokyo at this time?"

"No, not that I am aware of," replied the ambassador cautiously and then adding: "The last thing of any consequence was that shooting incident which injured two of my people here. They are both okay, but it seems to have been directed against us by local people objecting to that perennial Kurils problem. That should not really bother us or the CIA."

Then it went quiet as he paused to think and Bortsov was about to check if the line was still open when the ambassador continued: "But hold on a moment, Yuri. I have just remembered that the attache who was on the receiving end of a bullet was that man Aldanov. I know that he was one of your agents and you will remember that he was the one involved in that disastrous Russian Lieutenant business in England a couple of years ago. He made a big mistake and got sent here as a naval attache as a punishment and ended up in hospital".

The General laughed heartily at his own story, but Bortsov was not joining in. "Hold on a moment," he interrupted. "I think you may be on to something important. The CIA could well be interested in Aldanov. Has he recovered yet from his injury – is he back at work?"

"I think so," replied the ambassador. "I have not heard much about him lately, other than there is the court case coming up against the two shooters, which is being dealt as a local police issue. But I will check with your senior man here and let you know the latest."

"Yes, please," said Bortsov. "But don't raise an alarm. Can you just ask him to keep a very close eye on Aldanov's movements for a while please, very discretely. Find out who he meets outside. I will get back to you when I have checked a few things this end. Thank you for your time, Mr. Ambassador, I will be in touch."

Bortsov called his senior team together and briefed them on what Dubrinin had discovered about the woman agent's presence in Japan and how there could be a possible link with Aldanov at the Russian Embassy in Tokyo. "I don't know what the link is yet," he added. "But the CIA are on to something there and I want to find out more".

Meanwhile, at the Embassy in Japan, the ambassador sent for Pavel Livitsky, the head of the local GUR section, and asked him if he knew how Aldanov was settling in after the shooting incident.

"That was a bad start for him in his first week with us," replied Livitsy. "But he was lucky to get away with a gunshot wound in his shoulder and he was out of hospital after three or four days. He has been in and out of the office most days since then to check his in-box, and also going to the hospital for more treatment every few days. But Olga from admin has been mothering him so I have not seen much of him".

"Neither have I," said General Malinov. "On his first day back after the incident, I stopped by his office to ask how he was feeling and he reassured me that he would soon be fully recovered. Maybe I should have kept a bit closer, but nothing significant has cropped up in his sector. Anyway, I have just had an order from Moscow to keep a closer watch on his activities and I would like you to take this on, but very discretely. You know the story of his past when he was working with your people in Moscow, of course. Well, it sounds like something may have cropped up in connection with the woman who was involved, and that this could involve Aldanov in some way. I don't know any more yet – just this order to keep an eye on him. So I suggest you try to get to know him a bit better and find out what he is up to – and report back to me. Okay?".

"No problem and by the way, have you had any news on the other fellow, Endo?", asked the GRU chief. "He was a useful man to have around the place and we all used his local knowledge."

"I do see regular hospital reports," said the Ambassador. "He was quite seriously injured and our admin people are doing all they can to support him. As one of our employees, his care is covered by our insurance and it looks like continuing for some time. So when you talk to Aldanov, find out what he is doing about a replacement?"

Livitsky wasted no time. After returning to his own office to check for any urgent new business, he decided to visit the naval attache's office, but there was no sign of Nikolai Aldanov. So he moved on to the administration department and found Olga to ask: "How is Aldanov doing? I haven't seen him for a few days and I know you have been very kindly looking after his interests?"

"He's not a hundred per cent yet and I don't think his bosses in Moscow are putting any pressure on him," she replied. "He tends to come to his office in the mornings to deal with any current messages and updates, but he has not been to the Ambassador's weekly staff briefings yet. It seems that he goes off to the American Club for lunch most days and then rests at his apartment. I have planned to take him to visit Endo-san in the hospital tomorrow – but in general I think he feels embarrassed by the whole business of being involved in a bar shooting."

"I wonder why?" asked Livitsky, who realised that Olga probably had no knowledge of Aldanov's previous experiences, which probably accounted for his current attitude. He asked her to provide a follow up assessment on both men after her hospital visit the next day.

CHAPTER 23

IS IT HAL?

Samantha kept her phone by her during the morning as she tried to relax with a visit to the hotel exercise centre before breakfast. Next she went for a gentle swim in the pool where she was almost alone with her thoughts. She was in the coffee bar with the English language newspaper to take her mind off her concerns as noon approached when her phone rang at last. It was Georgina who asked quickly whether it would be convenient to come to the Hilton Hotel to share some further news? They agreed to meet in the lounge bar and Samantha found a quiet corner with two chairs to wait anxiously.

Georgina arrived in her military uniform about 15 minutes later and told Samantha that she had made an early start that morning in her office, reviewing the files of the communications department staff.

"The more I studied the records and thought about your question, my eyes kept returning to the same man," she said. "He's a bit different to the rest of them, rather introverted, often argumentative about small issues and also very frustrated about his lack of promotion," she began. "He is very smart, probably the brightest of the bunch, but never seems happy. He frequently applies for more senior positions and fails to understand why he is rejected. So is he the odd ball who may also be up to something else?"

Samantha was impressed. "That sounds like a good start. What else did you find?"

"Well, I began to wonder about him," continued Georgina. "Then I discovered that he is a single man with a Japanese girlfriend. He actually lives on base and does not seem to have any other special friends, interests or activities. He visits his girlfriend, mostly at weekends. Otherwise, he reads a lot of spy books, he watches movies for hours, and he studies foreign languages and apparently understands a good deal of Russian. How does that sound?"

Samantha listened intently, building up a mental picture of the man and then secretly crossed her fingers and asked hopefully: "What is this guy's name?"

"It's Halliburton - William Ash Halliburton," came the reply.

Trying to hide her surprise, Samantha asked calmly: "Do his pals call him William, Bill or maybe Hal?" She was half-expecting the answer and then went on to describe her encounter with an army man called Hal in the Hilton bar two evenings earlier. "He was strangely inquisitive about my reasons for visiting Okinawa, and he certainly matches your description of his personality" she added.

Realising that they had somehow identified a suspect, the two women began to consider what they should do next? Samantha said that her next move would be to report the identification of a suspicious individual to her boss and seek advice. They agreed that they did not have any real evidence to pursue and began to consider ways in which an operator in the Chatan base might be able to pass on secret information to Russia without being detected? They agreed that he could not send it electronically once a week without the risk of being intercepted, so maybe there was just an old-fashioned secret drop point and a local accomplice?

Georgina agreed to keep a closer eye on Hal and to stay in touch over the coming days. They confirmed their contact phone numbers before going their separate ways and Samantha realised that the ball was now in her court. When she returned to her hotel room, she decided to send a text message on the confidential link to Melanie: "Positive progress to report from inquiries made by my new contact".

CHAPTER 24

"THE RUSSIAN THING"

S amantha was back in her room after a light lunch when she answered another phone call from Melanie in Tokyo.

"Sorry to disturb you again. Are you alone now?" she began.

Getting a positive response, she went on to ask about the new developments from her army contact?"

Samantha described the details passed on to her earlier by Georgina and continued: "With that information and my own meetings in the hotel bar with the army people including this Halliburton man, I really think we are on to something important. I guess we have been a bit lucky to identify a suspect so quickly. What is our next move?"

Melanie congratulated Samantha and said she had done well, then went on: "First of all, your contact is a really good one – she is authentic and her bosses in Washington have confirmed that she is one of their stars in the intelligence section. If it turns out to be an army culprit, Georgina and her team can handle the next stages. Bob Smithers is still here and he has been getting more information from his cyber people and they are now piecing things together. His suggestion is that you should fly back to Tokyo today if possible and we can all have a review meeting first thing tomorrow. Can you do that?"

"Yes, of course," replied a surprised Samantha, "I will check flights right away and let you know my ETA. I imagine it will depend on a connecting flight from Osaka?"

"No, it's easier than that," said Melanie. "I have already checked it out and there are several direct flights from Naha to Tokyo. It is about three hours and then you will probably need another couple of hours to get here from Narita. I suggest you get the Airport Express train into the city, so just send me a message when you are on the way and I will know when to convene the meeting with Bob."

Samantha agreed and she was soon checking flights on line and booked a 1530 departure from Naha. But first she made a call to her army friend, Georgina, to let her know she had been recalled to Tokyo to review the situation with the chief from Washington. She then added: "But if you have any further thoughts about your man Hal, or anyone else who might be involved, do let me know. Whoever it is must have a link to the Russian embassy in Tokyo." Georgina said she understood and was clearly pleased to be involved in something different.

Samantha quickly packed her bag, checked out from the hotel and waited anxiously while the parking attendant retrieved her rental car from the underground garage. The drive to Naha airport and the car return depot formalities went smoothly and she was in the terminal building with just 30 minutes before the flight departure, time to grab a bagel and coffee.

As the aircraft flew north from Okinawa, she tried to relax and clear her thoughts from the brief stay in the island. She began to focus on her notes about the mission and to consider what might be the next moves. She now knew enough about the CIA and its operations to recognise that her recall to Tokyo at this stage was straight out of the Bob Smithers repertoire – putting two and two together to make five! In this case, it probably involved her past connection with Nikolai Aldanov. And although she had been determined to put "the Russian thing" behind her, she knew that she was unable to avoid it in the interests of this new threat to national security.

On the crowded Narita Express train by 7pm, she updated Melanie who confirmed that the briefing with Bob Smithers would be at the Embassy at 9am in the morning.

As a refreshed Samantha arrived in the Ambassador's top floor conference room, Bob Smithers was already there. "Hi, Sam. Great to see you again," he said as she walked in, smiling and confident. He gave her a hug and asked: "Did you have a good vacation in Okinawa?" Samantha laughed and replied: "Well, as you probably know, I've been quite busy and the place is full of Americans, mostly service people, so not where I would choose for a vacation."

After a few minutes, the three of them then began to discuss progress on their mission to discover the source of secret information leaks. Bob asked Samantha for more details about the contact she had made with the military intelligence officer and the possible suspect she had identified. He complimented her on discovering a helpful military intelligence officer and went on to update them on the progress made by analysts back at CIA headquarters. They had been able to verify the background details of Lieutenant Winters and also Sergeant Halliburton and had recommended that the line of inquiry was worth pursuing further. They had found that the timing pattern of the leaks certainly seemed to coincide with someone working shifts and they had now been able to pin down the actual dates and times when the codes had been intercepted.

"Can you ask your lady contact in Chatan whether these times actually coincide with the work pattern of her suspect?" asked Bob, passing to her a document with a series of dates and times. Samantha said this should be no problem and asked if they had any idea about how the information was being transmitted to Russia.

"Not yet," was the cautious reply. "But our guys have traced some signs of a carefully disguised satellite link which carries brief, intermittent transmissions between Okinawa and the embassy here. The transmission are very irregular and we suspect that they may be carrying the problem data in some way. But we need to dig a bit deeper and this is where you come in, Sam. We think there is one soft spot among the Russians here in Tokyo – a guy you know called Aldanov. You know he was injured in that shooting incident in a Tokyo bar a few weeks ago. Well, he is recovered now and back at work in the Russian embassy."

Samantha could see that coming. But she was apprehensive about what would happen next and how they proposed to make contact with him.

"I was thinking about this on my flight back," she said. "I can see several ways in which my first conversation with him might go. But how do I set about contacting him and then finding an opportunity to have a confidential talk?"

"That is why we wanted you here now," said Melanie. "It was Bob's idea for my guys here to use their contacts with the Japanese Security Service people for the trial of the two gunmen to begin today. Aldanov was scheduled to give evidence in the Tokyo court at the trial of the two gunmen who shot him and his sidekick. He is okay now, and they used an arrangement they have here for any witness who may be in some danger during a trial to be accommodated in a secure facility. So the trial is being opened today and then adjourned for a week or two. So Mr. Aldanov will be the guest of the Japanese police tonight and we have arranged to take you there to talk to him. I know it won't be easy for you, but I am sure you know what to do."

"Will I be on my own?" asked Samantha. "And what outcome are you looking for?"

"Well, ideally, we want him on our side", replied Bob, who went on to describe the plan whereby she would be taken to Aldanov's accommodation room later that evening. The room had been equipped with a hidden microphone, and he together with Melanie would be based nearby to record and listen to the conversation.

Samantha was impressed by the planning and decided not to ask too many questions. In her luggage, she found a more formal shirt and jacket which, together with some fresh make-up and some discreet jewellery gave her more confidence for the evening ahead. Soon the time came for them to go to the waiting limousine which drove them to the crucial rendezvous at the city courthouse. On the way, Bob did his best to amuse the two ladies with reminiscences from his previous trips to Tokyo and encounters with the city's night life. The traffic was busy but eventually they arrived at a modern two-storey block and adjoining it was one of the city's more remote police stations where they were greeted by a senior officer from the Japanese PSIA organisation.

After a brief discussion in the small office, it was time for action and Bob's final words were: "I am sure you know how to play this one, Sam. There is no hurry so take your time to win him over – again!"

CHAPTER 25
WHERE IS NIKOLAI?

During the same afternoon, a couple of miles away at the Russian Embassy, Ambassador Malinov was having another briefing from his GRU Station chief Pavel Livitsky and asked: "So, have you discovered what Aldanov is doing yet?"

"Not very much, it seems," came the reply. "Two of my agents have stayed on his tail since you gave us the task and his routine seems to be to walk from his apartment to the office every morning, check his mail and on-line messages and then chat with Olga in the admin office who is trying to find him an assistant to replace Endo. He then sits at his desk and reads files until mid-day and then gets the metro to the American club where he chats to different people and has lunch – pretty boring, it seems."

Livitsky went on to describe how for the rest of the day, it seemed that Aldanov either went sightseeing in the city or returned to his apartment for quiet evenings with his TV and his books. And his phone and on-line records showed nothing of concern.

"I must say that sounds a bit out of character for a man who was so active as a GRU agent, even if he did blot his copybook. So who does he chat to at the Club? Any women among them?" asked the General.

"My guys tried to check this and they could not find any pattern or repeated contacts, male or female," said Livitsky. "So I went there myself yesterday and the only difference was that when he spotted me, he came to join me in the bar. As we chatted, it seems that he is getting restless about having very little to do now that he has stopped having regular treatment at the hospital. He has visited Endo at the hospital a couple of times, but otherwise the only other excitement he mentioned were a couple of sessions with the local police to give them statements and to answer other questions about that shooting in the bar".

The Ambassador thought about it for a moment and said that the people in Moscow were probably giving him time to settle in and fully recover before sending him any new assignments. Then he asked: "You mentioned the police inquiries. Will the two guys they arrested be going on trial any time soon? If so, Aldanov will have to give evidence so perhaps we should find an opportunity to have a briefing with him about what he can and cannot say about his job here."

Livinsky said he would check this out and report back.

He was back within an hour. "Your instinct was spot on, General", he said. "We have just discovered that the trial of the two Japanese gunmen has actually started today at the city courthouse and a car collected Aldanov this morning to take him there. I have sent one of my guys to the court buildings to try to discover what is going on and to make contact with Aldanov. I will let you know as soon as I hear more."

General Malinov banged his fist angrily on his desk, stood up and shouted at Livitsy: "What the hell is going on here? What has happened to normal protocol? We should have had notice of this so that we can have legal advice and…"

He marched out to find his assistant in the outer office and instructed her firmly: "Call the foreign ministry at once and tell Mr. whatshisname I need an urgent appointment now, and I mean NOW."

She knew that he meant Mr. Masuko, his usual contact at the ministry and he was on the line within a few minutes. Although she was unable to tell him the subject of the meeting, he soon recognised from her insistence that it was an urgent matter and he was able to confirm a 4pm meeting that afternoon with a deputy minister in the department for international relations. She booked the car and driver immediately and returned to the Ambassador's office with the information.

The Ambassador quickly decided to take Pavel Livinsky with him and he was pensive during the 30 minutes journey to the government complex in the Chiyoda-ku district of the city, saying very little and checking the time on his watch every few minutes. Livinsky took a call on his mobile phone and then reported to the General: "That was the man I sent to the court to make contact with Aldanov. He says that case was opened by the judge this afternoon and that after an opening statement from the prosecuting counsel it was adjourned for a week, apparently because arrangements have to be made to take evidence from Endo at the hospital. My agent says there was no sign of Aldanov, who was not called as a witness today. And he has not yet returned to his office or his apartment."

The Ambassador was still trying to understand this news when they arrived with a few minutes to spare and he was relieved to find his contact waiting in the reception area of the ministry building. "Masuko-san, so good to see you again," said the General, returning the polite welcoming bow. "Thank you so much for arranging this appointment at such short notice."

"My pleasure, Mr. Ambassador," said the Japanese officlal, bowing even lower. "Please to follow me."

The lift took them to the second floor and a maze of corridors until they reached the spacious and elegant office of Mr. Takahashi, a minister in the foreign affairs division who was in charge of liaison with overseas embassies. He knew the Russian ambassador from previous meetings and functions and greeted him warmly. After the traditional bowing, the General introduced Pavel Livinsky as his chief of military intelligence and said how grateful he was for the minister's time at such short notice.

The minister returned to the swivel chair behind his large desk and indicated that his visitors should take their seats facing him and said rather formally: "I am sure it must be a matter of some importance, Malinov-san. So how can I be of assistance?"

"Yes, it is a matter relating to that shooting incident a few weeks ago in the Ginza when two of my Embassy staff were injured, as I am sure you remember," began the General. "One of them is still in hospital but the other man, Aldanov, was not seriously injured and he is now back at work. This afternoon, I learned that Mr. Aldanov had been taken by a police vehicle from the

Russian embassy to the city courthouse where the two assailants are apparently on trial. Aldanov is a witness as well as a victim, of course, but we were not accorded the usual courtesy of advance information about the start of the trial or the requirement for Aldanov to give evidence today".

"I see", said the minister. "If we failed to inform you, I can only apologise, but the court proceedings would not be a matter under the control of this ministry. It would be under the aegis of the home affairs ministry and the security and intelligence division. I will certainly take it up with them on your behalf immediately."

"This is important to us, minister," said the General. "It is also a security matter for us, which is why I have Mr. Livitsky here with me. I will tell you in confidence that the man involved, Aldanov, is a former GRU agent. If we had known about the start of the trial, we would have had the opportunity to brief him and send him to the court with a lawyer who could explain your procedures and advise him. That would be normal in a foreign country".

Mr. Takahashi took careful notes and then responded, as he stood up to indicate that the brief meeting was over: "Yes, I agree that there has been an oversight here. I will investigate this matter as soon as possible and contact you again tomorrow".

The two Russians also stood up, but the Ambassador insisted: "I would like an answer tonight, it you please? I am told that Aldanov has not returned to the embassy or to his apartment and I am very concerned in the circumstances. If you have any information, please ask Masuko-san to contact me at any time. He knows how to find me."

The minister nodded to show his understanding as they all bowed again and the visitors left his office, somewhat perplexed.

CHAPTER 26

A SURPRISE VISITOR

A rather bewildered Nikolai Aldanov sat on the edge of the single bed in his small room at the police station and reflected on a strange and unexpected day. It was about mid-day when he had a call in his office to go to the embassy entrance lobby where he was greeted by a uniformed police officer and another man in civilian clothes who introduced himself as officer Noriaki from the PSIA security department.

"I apologise for not speaking Russian, Mr. Aldanov, but I understand that you also speak some English like me," began the officer. "We are very pleased that you are now recovered and back at work and would like you to come with us for another short meeting to discuss the evidence you will be giving at the trial of the gunmen who injured you. It will not take long."

They were already escorting him through the door to a waiting car before he had time to respond, other than to call out to the reception desk to inform Olga that he had gone to a meeting with the police. When he had visited his assistant Endo at the hospital a couple of days earlier, he had been told of a visit which the police had made to the hospital to discuss with Endo when he might be well enough to give evidence at a future trial. So the call to collect him at the embassy did not come as a complete surprise. The surprise came on the way when Noriaki explained that they were actually going to the courthouse where a judge would be opening the trial that afternoon and that he might be called to give evidence.

"It will all be in Japanese," said Mr.Noriaki. "But I will be with you as your interpreter."

In the courtroom, Aldanov and his interpreter were seated at the back of the very formal room and after a short wait, the proceedings began. He understood none of it but had the opportunity to watch the two accused who were in the dock with armed guards. Both looked rather young and innocent, he thought. Occasionally, Noriaki whispered in his ear, explaining that the judge was hearing the details of the indictment from the prosecuting attorney and discussing how to take evidence from the victim who was still in hospital – or whether to delay the trial. Issues were then raised by the defence lawyer and it was clearly taking a long time to resolve. After nearly two hours, the hearing was adjourned, and it was explained to Aldanov that it would resume again the next morning when he would be called to give evidence. As they left the courtroom together, there was yet another surprise when it was explained to him that because of the risk of an important witness being contacted or influenced by another party, he would be given an overnight safe room in the adjoining police hostel.

He was relieved to find that it was more like a small hotel than a police department. Noriaki led him to a first floor room which was small but comfortably furnished with a single bed, an arm chair and TV set, a small table and chair and an adjoining private bathroom with a shower. On the table was a colourful bento-box containing a selection of Japanese delicacies together with a coffee machine and bottles of water. And on the bed was a small travel bag which, as he later discovered, contained toiletries including a razor, plus a kimono-style night-shirt. There was a dinner menu, but his escort told him he could use the police canteen in the adjoining building if he preferred.

As he settled in and tried to relax, he could not help asking himself what facilities the Russian authorities would provide in similar circumstances – probably a bare police cell. But his thoughts were interrupted by a knock on his door and the voice of his interpreter: "Mr. Aldanov, you have a visitor. It is a lady and is it convenient for her to come in please?"

Aldanov opened his door and was surprised to see a very smart, blonde woman who quickly stepped inside and said: "*Dobry vecher – kek dela*?" as she took his hand and added "Me – Samantha". He was uncertain about his unexpected visitor and wondered whether this part of his welcome package was in fact a call girl. He greeted her rather cautiously but then gave her a welcoming smile: "I also speak English – me Nikolai. Can I help you?"

"Well actually, I am here to help you – can I sit down for a chat… in English please?"

"Yes, of course", he said, indicating the armchair as he quickly tidied away his belongings. When he sat down opposite her, he had a sudden flash of recognition and added: "Have we met before somewhere? You sound American".

Quickly deciding to waste no time she replied: "Yes, in fact we have met but it is a long story. Do you remember arriving in Portsmouth on board a navy ship nearly two years ago and then meeting a woman on the dockside?" she asked. Aldanov thought for a moment and looked at her closely before replying: "Of course I remember that day and it cost me my job. But that was not you, was it?"

Samantha told him that she would explain more about that later and added: "But first it will be helpful if you can tell me what you remember about the things that happened before and after that meeting?"

"It was not good", he recalled. "I was arrested and sent to an English jail for a month and then I was flown back to Russia to be reprimanded and fired from my job with the GUR which I was really enjoying. And that was after I had successfully tracked down a potential new contact in Britain."

"So what happened to you next?" she answered. He looked searchingly at her and thought for a few moments before continuing: "I remember reading reports in Moscow which said that the woman had died from some sort of poisoning and that there was a naval funeral. Apparently one of my London colleagues sent a red rose from me which made headlines. That did not go down well with the bosses either and I was soon moved to a boring desk job in the defence ministry. Then, after a few months, I was sent here to a dead-end posting in Japan where not much happens, only to be shot by a crazy gunman in my first week. So it was not a happy episode."

"It wasn't happy for the woman who was poisoned either, was it?" she countered. "Or for her family and her friends. What did you feel about that?"

Aldanov just shook his head, rather dismissively, as Samantha looked into his eyes and told him, slowly and deliberately: "You were part of a GUR death squad. You began by making Marina Peters believe she had a romantic relationship with a Russian navy lieutenant, then went too far when you met her and made the mistakes which led to your arrest. Your team then tried to cover up your stupid actions by silencing Marina, the only witness, before you could be put on trial to explain yourself. That is all true, isn't it?"

"And so what," replied Aldanov coldly.

Samantha stood up and his eyes followed her as she moved slowly round the small room. "This is what," she said firmly. "You owe me – you owe me big time. Because yes, I was Marina Peters. That was me. So let me tell you what really happened next."

He looked shocked, then disbelieving, as she went on to describe in painful detail how Ricin poison had been left in her mailbox by two Russian agents; and then how she had been given only a slender chance of survival – until she became a guinea pig for a new Ricin antidote developed in America. She described how a plan was created to arrange a mock funeral in case the antidote was unsuccessful – but to create a "new Marina" if she survived.

Aldanov became pensive at this and he began to listen quietly as she spelt out details of her three months of treatment at an American military hospital and the wonderful care she had received from doctors and psychologists. She said this had worked so well that she was flown secretly to Washington to be given a new American identity as Samantha Lord and eventually launched into a new career as a secret agent.

He began to realise that he was now talking to "the other side" and could be in danger if this was discovered. Now she had his full attention as she went on to describe the heartache of making the decision to embark on this new life which also meant being unable to see her family and former friends again. She added that as a former GUR agent himself, he would certainly understand the separate world in which the secret services of their countries operated and the importance of national security.

"So now do you understand why you thought we had met previously?" she finally asked Aldanov, who was now looking somewhat chastened by her story.

"Ok Marina, or Samantha, whichever you are," he said becoming more sympathetic. "I had no idea about all this and as you said a while ago, I guess I owe you. So what can I do?"

In the nearby administrative office, Bob Smithers and Melanie had been listening attentively and at this point, they looked at eachother. "Wow, she's quite some lady" said Bob, and Melanie added: "You said it - that questioning was quite forensic - worthy of a top lawyer."

They continued to listen as Samantha went on: "You have some good experience of how GRU operates and you said that you missed working as an agent, so for starters here's an opportunity to do something about it. I am working on an assignment here and I need some inside information from your embassy. Someone there is receiving highly secret information about once a week from an American military contact in Okinawa and passing it on to Moscow. There is a senior man from the CIA headquarters in the states here in Tokyo now to work on this and we just want to track the source. Could you do this?"

Nikolai Aldanov looked astonished at first, but then his demeanour slowly brightened. He seemed to be flattered to think that his real talent had been recognised again – even by "the other side" – and he asked how soon this information was needed. He then explained: "Our GUR team here is quite small, just four or five people, and I am not part of it, of course. But it should not be too difficult to work out which one of them has such a good US contact – can you give me a week? I still have to clear up this Japanese court business first, I guess."

"Of course, Nikolai, but just think about it for a few minutes," replied Samantha, deciding to become less formal with him for the first time. "I need a bathroom break and will be back in a few minutes."

She went to find her CIA colleagues who greeted her with hugs and congratulations. "We heard it all and you were brilliant," said Bob. "So what happens next?" she asked. "Do you want to meet him now? It would probably reassure him to know that he has authority from someone senior?"

Bob and Melanie looked at each other thoughtfully and Bob shook his head slowly, which was the cue for Melanie to respond: "It is your assignment, Sam, so just go with it. You can tell him you have called your manager and reported on your conversation and his willingness to co-operate. I think the next stage now is for you to arrange a follow up contact and send him on his way".

"Yep, that's about it, Sam, so keep up the good work," Bob added. "And by the way, I have some more surprise news for you. Your friend Tom Spencer from London is visiting the British embassy here this week and says he is hoping to see you."

The news about Tom's visit put a spring in Samantha's step as she returned to Aldanov's room. She told him that her director was delighted with the outcome of their discussion and that she would look forward to meeting him again when he had some information to share. She gave him her mobile phone number and suggested that he should call her from a public pay phone when he was ready – and to also suggest a suitable discrete rendezvous.

As she left, she could sense from his comments and demeanour that he was feeling rather pleased to be back in the spy business again. She then found that Bob and Melanie had already left the building so she called a taxi to return to her flat – realising as she tried to relax that it had been a long and exhausting day.

CHAPTER 27

THE TRIAL BEGINS

Nikolai Aldanov had a disturbed night as he recalled the details of his surprise evening visitor and decided that she was actually rather attractive. He was awake and still considering his next move when there was another knock on his door. This time, it was his English-speaking Japanese police escort who offered to take him to the canteen for breakfast and added: "But first there is a Russian gentleman in reception asking for you, and a message from the court officer to tell you that the trial resumes at 9.30 and that you will be the first witness."

He showered and dressed as quickly as possible, wondering who his next visitor might be? He was surprised again to find it was Ilia, one of the agents from the GUR section at the Russian embassy. "We lost you yesterday," he said. "And it took us a while to track you down. The only clue we had was from our security man who said you had been driven away in a police car. So we had no idea what was happening."

"I'm sorry about that," replied Nikolai. "I told the doorman to inform Olga when I left – perhaps he forgot. So why were you checking up on me?" asked Nikolai. "I am here for the trial of those two gunmen who shot me and Endo. It all starts in an hour or so and I have to deal with all this before I can get down to my proper job."

"Okay, I think I understand now," replied the agent. "But it is not every day that one of our officers is driven away from the embassy by the police without the admin people knowing. Let's have a cup of coffee and a chat."

The Japanese police escort was standing by and he led them both to the adjoining entrance to the police canteen where they had time for coffee and a hot dog while Nikolai explained his experience in the courtroom the previous afternoon and the reason for his overnight stay in the hostel. They agreed that they just had to accept that it was the Japanese ways of doing such things – and went on to chat about life at the embassy. Eventually, Nikolai was called to go to the adjoining courtroom and Ilia took the opportunity to call his boss, who instructed him to stay with Aldanov now that they had found him.

From a back seat in the public area of the modern, wood-panelled courtroom, he watched in fascination as the formalities of the court hearing began, but not understanding it. The two accused men were being closely guarded in the dock and after lengthy statements from men he assumed were the attorneys, the judge gave an instruction and an officer called out the name of Nikolai Aldanov. A young female interpreter stood alongside the witness box and she began to interpret each stage of the proceedings in Russian, so Ilia began to pay attention.

In reply to questions from the prosecuting attorney, Nikolai said he could not identify the two men in the dock and was not aware that he and his colleague may have been followed to the café. He had seen nothing to alarm him before he heard the gunshots and realised that both he and Endo had been injured. In the melee which followed, he was only grateful for the help they received from other customers and the staff until the medical help arrived. In reply to a question, he said he could think of no reason why they should have been targeted by gunmen. He also explained that it was the end of his first week in Japan in a new posting to the Russian embassy. Endo had been showing him round parts of Tokyo for the first time, so he was unfamiliar with the surroundings.

The defending attorney pursued the question of recognition and it appeared to Ilia that he was suggesting that Aldanov's testimony did not incriminate the two accused men, who had just been two among a large crowd of customers in the bar at the time. There was further lengthy dialogue between the judge and the attorneys and then a statement by the judge which was interpreted to inform Aldanov that he was now discharged as a witness and that the trial would be adjourned until Endo was fit to give evidence.

A relieved Nikolai was pleased to see Ilia waiting for him outside the courtroom and they took a taxi for the 30-minute drive back to the Embassy. On the way, it was an opportunity for Nikolai to develop a closer relationship with Ilia and to start sharing stories from their experiences as GUR agents – and to ask casually whether he had any contacts with the American military in Japan. "Not yet," he replied. "But it is an important area for our group and Mikhail has been here the longest and he seems to get involved with some useful connections in the US army. I gather it is a productive area for information."

"Yes, I was involved in the same thing in my days in Moscow," confided Nikolai. "Because I had served in the navy, one of my jobs was to target the British navy and I uncovered one very good new contact – did you hear about how it got me into trouble?"

"Not really," said Ilia. "But I understand that there was some woman trouble which upset the bosses – but everyone makes mistakes in this business and I have heard many worse cases, so don't worry".

As they arrived back at the embassy, Nikolai recognised that he had found a good contact in the youngest member of the local GUR team – though probably not the right one. So what next?

Back at his office desk the next morning, he decided to spread the word that his involvement in the shooting trial was over and that he was ready to work on his real job, starting with his in-box of messages from Moscow. But first, he called on Olga and asked about the arrangements for finding a replacement for Endo – temporary or permanent. She had a file ready for him, with resumes from six applicants for support jobs at the Embassy. "Start with these," she suggested. "Then come and talk about anyone who looks interesting."

He then moved on to visit the information department and asked Veronika to look for any coverage of the trial of the two Japanese gunmen and make him a copy – especially if it reached the Russian media. Then he decided to let the Ambassador's assistant know that he was now back at his desk and would be at the next weekly briefing. Finally, he went to the office occupied by the GUR agents – the Intelligence Section – and greeted Ilia at his desk. "Hello again. Do you have time to get lunch at the sushi bar?" he asked. They agreed to meet in the lobby at 12.30.

As they chatted over their Japanese bento boxes and joked about their inexperience with chopsticks, Nikolai told Ilia how much he wanted to get back to working in the GUR again. "The Ambassador advised me to stay clear of anything to do with your department," he explained. "But I am sure you understand how I feel."

Ilia agreed. "Once a spook, always a spook," he commented, with a laugh and asked how he could help his new friend.

Nikolai continued: "I think it might help me if word went back direct to your bosses in Moscow, perhaps through Pavel Livitsky, that I had been useful in some way. What do you think?"

Ilia nodded his agreement and his new friend continued: "It's like this. When I was in the American club a couple of days ago, I heard someone saying that a top man from the CIA in the States is staying there for a few days, so I tried hard to hear more of the conversation", said Nikolai. "I could not get it all, but it seemed like he has a team trying to locate our man in Okinawa who gets info from American military sources. Does that make sense to you?"

"Well yes. I know this is one of the areas that Mikhail handles," said Ilia, becoming intrigued. "I am not familiar with the details but I do know that he makes contact with a Russian immigrant in Okinawa who works near one of the army bases there. Does that make sense to you?"

"I have no idea," Nikolai continued. "I don't even know where Okinawa is, but I was told in my briefing that there is a great deal of the American military based here in Japan. Why not give it a thought for a few days and maybe then mention to your boss Livitsky that you were having a chat with me and that I told you about a top CIA man being at the American club – which of course, he probably knows already. If it sounds like he wants to follow up with me, tell him you are sure I would be happy to talk to him."

They paid for their lunch and the subject was not mentioned again as they walked back to the Embassy.

Later in the day, on his way back to his apartment, Nikolai found a pay-phone and called the number Samantha had given him. "I have some new information about Okinawa," he told her and they quickly arranged a discrete rendezvous in a nearby park for 8am the next day.

CHAPTER 28

A DOUBLE AGENT?

I t was a cool, sunny morning and Samantha found a convenient park bench to watch the colourful scene as more than fifty local people, men and women, were going through their *rajio taiso* calisthenics programme as they listened to radio music – a regular routine before starting work. She was almost tempted to join in when Nikolai arrived and greeted her cheerfully – "Found you," he said. "Lovely morning."

They were discussing the impressive exercise routines when, to Nikolai's surprise, they were joined by a tall man in his 50's, wearing a sweater, blue jeans, dark glasses and baseball cap. "Can I join you, I'm Bob", he said with a friendly Texan drawl. "Yes, this is my boss from America," Samantha added quickly, by way of explanation.

"So you are the famous Russian lieutenant who created so much trouble for this lady, and for me," Bob Smithers began. "I have heard a lot about you and never thought I would actually meet you, not least here in Tokyo of all places. How do you like your new job here?".

"Not very much," replied Nikolai, rather sadly in his Russian-accented English. "Samantha has told me all about it and I am really sorry for all the problems I caused for you both."

"And for lots of other people, too," Bob added, sternly. Then he continued: "But I understand from Samantha, or is it Marina, that you may be able to help us now in some way? You probably know how this business works as well as I do from your time in GUR, so maybe there are things we can talk about. Are you interested?"

Then looking around the area, he asked quietly: "Do you think you are being followed? Don't look now but behind the tree along the footpath is a man with a camera who seems to be taking an interest in us. I don't like the look of him. You must know that if your people discover that you have been meeting here with us, you will be in great trouble – probably on the first plane to Moscow and then who knows what? A gulag, or worse? Do you want me to get you out of this? Tell me quickly…"

Aldanov looked frightened and just nodded his agreement… but before he could speak, two uniformed Japanese police officers were approaching along the footpath and Bob gave them a pre-arranged signal. To the astonishment of others nearby watching the calisthenics, the policemen immediately escorted the three of them from the park bench to a waiting limousine on the road just a few yards away, which then sped off into the traffic. The watching man ran out from his hiding place but did not even have time to take another photograph before quickly calling the Russian embassy to report on what he had seen.

Nothing further was said as Bob Smithers, Samantha and a bewildered Nikolai Aldanov were being driven to the American Embassy where a private room in the Security section was awaiting them. They were brought coffee and cookies, and as they began to relax, Nikolai asked: "So what happens now?"

Bob replied: "Well, in your chat with our lovely lady here, she got the impression that you were missing the excitement of working in the GUR and might be able to help us? Actually, we are trying to locate a particular Russian informant in Okinawa who is breaching our security. I had worked out a plan in which you might have helped us with this inquiry while continuing in your position as naval attache - a sort of double agent. But that option is shot now if there is a chance that you were followed this morning and were probably photographed talking with us. So it looks as though you are now on our side."

"Yes, I guess so, but what do you want me to do and where? There are not many options I can think of," replied Nikolai.

Bob said he was thinking… and he suddenly went out of the room, leaving Nikolai and Samantha to chat but they carefully avoided saying more about the crucial subject as they poured a second cup of coffee – and wondered when breakfast would be available? After ten minutes or so, Bob returned together with his Tokyo Station chief, Melanie Mackintosh and – much to Samantha's amazement – Tom Spencer from MI5 in London.

"I just heard you were in town and this is a big surprise" said Samantha as Tom greeted her with a warm hug. "It's so good to see you again," he replied.

After the two new arrivals had been introduced to the Russian, Tom recalled with a grin that he had met Nikolai once before, when he had interviewed him in his naval uniform in Portsmouth. "A lot has happened to us all since then," he added.

Bob then surprised Samantha by taking a more friendly approach to the Russian as he explained: "Okay, Nikolai. Let me tell you more. I think we can have you stay here quietly for a few days to see how we get on with our current assignment, maybe with your help. Your people will make a big fuss and try to find you, of course, but we will deny everything. We can give you a room in the embassy for a few days while we sort things out. We will fix up some toiletries and clean clothes and anything else you might need".

Aldanov looked surprised and worried, but Bob then added with a grin: "It will be a bit more comfortable than anything you would get back in Moscow. So looking further ahead, if all goes well I think we can arrange to ship you out secretly on a military plane to either the UK or to the States. We can give you a new identity and then some training with our folks. At least your English is good and you know something about our business. We will find you a quiet desk job for a while. Then later on, if all goes well, we might even send you out to work as an agent in some part of the world where speaking and understanding Russian will be useful. So you would be back in the spy business again. How does that sound?"

Nikolai shook his head slowly and said it was a lot to take in. But he said he understood and could probably get used to the new situation in time. He was still thinking it through and it came as a relief when Melanie interrupted with the suggestion that they should all go to the private dining room on the next floor where they would go on chatting over some breakfast.

CHAPTER 29

A SURPRISE DINNER DATE

After a relaxed thirty minutes exchanging light conversation over breakfast, mostly about the differences between the CIA and MI5, Bob said it was time to take his British counterpart away for a planned meeting with the Ambassador. Melanie made a call to Mary-Jo in the administration department asking her to join them and when she arrived Nikolai was introduced as an important visitor who would be staying in one of the embassy guest rooms for a few nights. This was not a surprise request from the head of the CIA section, but it was more unusual to be asked to arrange for all his needs – including toiletries and spare clothes as well as organising meals and emphasising that he would not be leaving the embassy building for any reason.

Mary-Jo was pleased to see that Nikolai happily agreed with these arrangements and that he also spoke to her in good English as they left the dining room together.

When she was eventually alone with Samantha, Melanie could not resist her curiosity any longer and asked: "Tell me more about Tom Spencer from

London? He's rather nice and you have obviously met him before. Why is he here in Tokyo?"

"I have no idea why he is here," said Samantha. "But yes, I met him a few times when we were working on a joint CIA and MI5 project and I had to arrange a couple of briefings for him in Langley. He is quite senior, you know – Deputy Director of Operations in London, I think, so I guess he is at Bob Smithers level. And yes, you are right, he is rather nice… in a sort of quiet British way."

Melanie gave an understanding smile and added: "So he knew Nikolai as well. That was another surprise. Small world, I guess. Maybe that has something to do with why he is here? Anyway, I guess all will be revealed in due course and meanwhile we have some work to do. So let's get on and can I suggest you start by following up with your Army contact in Okinawa and tell her what the Russian man said about the connection there."

Back at her desk in the CIA operations room, Samantha lost no time in calling the number she had been given by Army Lieutenant Georgina Winters. She had to leave a discrete recorded message and waited for a return call. It did not take long.

"Good to hear from you," said Georgina. "What's going on there in Tokyo?"

Samantha went on to explain in detail how the CIA now had a reliable informant at the Russian embassy who had confirmed that one of the GUR agents in Tokyo had an operational contact in Okinawa. He had been described as probably a Russian immigrant to Japan who now had a job of some sort in the tourism business. "We will try to get more details", she added.

"But this does seem to tick a couple of boxes and maybe you can also check whether any of your locally engaged people have a Russian background and could be in contact with your man Halliburton?"

"Hold on a moment," Georgina interrupted. "I don't think we would take on any locals here with a Russian background and certainly not in a sensitive area like communications. In fact, the locals we bring in are mainly cleaners and outside maintenance workers, but I will take a look at our personnel files to see if there are any clues there."

"Good idea," said Samantha. "But it may not be an insider link? It could be someone outside with Russian connections or sympathies who meets up with your man from time to time to receive information which they then pass on to the embassy in Tokyo. It may not involve new technology at all – just sending a personal text message or even a letter in the mail. Do you have the resources to put a trail on your suspect when he goes off duty to see who he meets or where he might drop off a hidden message? And another thing – our techies have worked out that the information from Okinawa seems to reach Tokyo and Moscow mainly at weekends."

"I can see why you work for the CIA and I am in the Army," said Georgina with a chuckle. "As it happens, I have one other officer here with security clearance who I can share some of this with. In fact, I think we might rather enjoy being sleuths. Can you give me a couple of days to follow up? I will stay in touch and let you know if we are making any progress."

Following this call, Samantha reported back to Melanie with an outline of her conversation and then returned to her desk to write up a record of her progress so far. Melanie said she would brief Bob Smithers when he became available and that they would review the situation again later. As she sat down, Samantha found a sealed envelope in her in-tray marked "personal" and opened it to find a hand-written note from Tom Spencer:

Dear Marina. So good to see you again, looking well and clearly enjoying the challenges of your new role. Can you get away in time to have dinner with me this evening and escape from work for a while? Let us say about 8pm at the Fukagawa Geisha Restaurant – any taxi driver will know how to find it. Tom XX

PS - if you have a problem just leave a vague message for me with Clare Hatfield at the British Embassy before 5pm today and I will contact you again tomorrow.

With feelings ranging from excitement to trepidation, Samantha quickly put the letter into her handbag and tried to focus on the challenge of her Okinawa mission. Could she really crack the crucial link with the help of her contact? Was there anything else she should or could do? She decided to talk to Mary-Jo and find out where to go to speak to Nikolai Aldanov again and was taken to a block of rooms at the back of the embassy where, it was explained to her, members of staff stayed when they were working late on important business. She indicated door number 4 and in response to her knock, she heard his call to "come on in."

It was a modern, two-roomed suite and she found him relaxing and watching television, seemingly untroubled by the dramatic events of the day. "This is nice," he said cheerfully, by way of a welcome. "I am enjoying having the Americans look after me, so I hope it lasts. Your boss was right. I won't find anything like this in Russia."

She apologised for interrupting him but explained that she really needed to ask more questions following their previous discussion. "Can you recall or discover any more details about the contact you mentioned in Okinawa," she asked. He went over his recollections of the earlier conversation with Ilia and seemed committed to her plan to track down the Russian informant. In conclusion, he said to her: "I have an idea. Let me get on the phone and talk to Ilia again."

He soon had his Russian colleague on the line and using the speakerphone so that Samantha could hear the conversation, he told him: "This is a bit difficult but on my way to the office this morning, I was surprised to be intercepted by an American in a car and brought here to the US Embassy. I think they believe that after all that has happened to me, I might be a soft touch for some information about the spook in Okinawa. You said something about your colleague Mikhail having a contact there so if you could find out a bit more for me, I think that would keep the CIA man happy and they will send me on my way."

Ilia thought for a moment before replying cautiously: "I am not sure what else I can do. Mikhail does not share this sort of information. I think he once said he had been to Okinawa on vacation a couple of times and I do recall him saying that his contact there had helped to find somewhere nice for his family to stay near the beach."

"That's interesting," said Nikolai. "So why not tell Mikhail that you want to take a holiday in Okinawa while the weather there is still warm and ask him if he can suggest someone to contact for more suggestions about hotels and the like? Oh and try to get the man's name."

"If it helps you, I'll give it a go," said Ilia. "Can I get back to you on this phone number?"

"Sure thing – good luck," said Nikolai, closing down the call.

Samantha told him this had been a good idea and said he should call her mobile number if he heard anything further. Meanwhile, she needed to return to her office and update Melanie who convened a follow up session with Bob Smithers. After Samantha had reported on her progress, Melanie suggested a call to her personal contact in the intelligence section of the Japanese foreign office and reached him in a few minutes.

After a few introductory words, she asked him: "We are trying to locate a possible Russian informant in Okinawa and it occurs to me that you may have an active watch list of individuals there with Russian connections - probably someone in the Chatan area, possibly involved in the holiday business or maybe working in some way with the American military."

She was on her speakerphone and the group was impressed with the efficiency of their Japanese counterparts as he told them he was already scanning a database with that information. He quickly came up with two results – both were Russian-sounding names of men who had apparently married Chinese wives and become Japanese nationals more than 10 years ago. He provided their residential addresses but added that neither man was identified as a special risk. He offered to alert a PSIA officer based in Chatan if any follow up was needed.

Melanie was hugely appreciative to her contact and said she would call again if further help was needed – but she could see from his gestures that Bob was eager to keep control of the inquiries. When the call ended, he told Samantha to pass on this new information to her military contact in Okinawa and to be ready to return there to follow up if necessary.

Another call to Georgina Winters set the wheels in motion. She was excited to hear the further details and insisted that she fully understood the implications. She said that with her army colleague, they would follow up in the next 24 hours – and Samantha waited nervously at her desk hoping that a return trip to Okinawa could at least wait until the following day.

But in just a couple of hours, an excited Georgina was back on the line. "We've got him," she said. "Your tip-off was spot on and we soon tracked the addresses of two Russian contacts you gave us – and believe it or not, we actually caught Halliburton in the act of handing over a sealed envelope to one of them. He is now in military custody here, saying very little but our legal affairs people will be taking over and they will liaise with you over the next day or two. Okay?"

"Fantastic news - well done," said Samantha and after a few more appreciative words, she went to find Bob Smithers in Melanie's office and shared the details. They were surprised and delighted and congratulated Samantha warmly for another success in her new career.

Bob then told them: "This is great timing so I will now leave it to you two to do the follow up stuff. I have a new crisis back in Langley and my plane will be taking me back to the States from the air force base here early tomorrow. So Melanie, can you arrange for a military escort to bring Aldanov to the base by 6am ready to fly with me and we will sort him out when we get to the States. Job done, I think."

CHAPTER 30

ANOTHER NEW NAME!

B ack in her apartment that evening, an exhilarated
Samantha decided that her first task should be a
quick check on Google about her date with Tom Spencer.
She was relieved to find that the geisha restaurant in
his letter was very much an up-market and traditional
example of this part of Japanese culture and not to be
confused with the more seamy bar-room gossip about
available geisha girls. She booked a taxi for 7.30 and her
next question was what to wear for such an occasion?
She had not yet had much opportunity for clothes
shopping, and she knew from her few experiences so
far that formal dining in Japan often required squatting
with crossed legs at a low table.

From her limited travel wardrobe, she was able to
find a smart pair of black palazzo pants to partner with
an emerald silk blouse, plus black high-heeled shoes
and to keep it simple she added just her favourite silver
stud earrings. As she twirled in front of her mirror,
she was quite impressed by the transformation and
hoped it would suit the occasion. The taxi arrived on
time and the driver nodded silently as he understood
the name of the Fukagawa Geisha Restaurant and sped

off into the bright lights of the city. Some 20 minutes later Samantha saw the name over the muted and rather formal entrance, contrasting with the garish lighting of nearby establishments. As the car pulled up, a uniformed attendant opened the door and bowed as he welcomed her by saying in perfect English: "Mr. Spencer is awaiting you madam."

He led her inside and Samantha was wide-eyed as they walked into the elegantly decorated and spacious room with discretely located low level tables set for two or four people, separated by colourful screens and with soft lighting. Most tables were occupied by Japanese diners, with just three or four who appeared to be Europeans and she could see only two other women. Gliding silently around the spacious room was the uniquely Japanese sight of at least a dozen beautiful geishas in their colourful floor length kimonos and sashes and with traditional hair styles decorated with flowers. She was so distracted that she did not notice Tom, standing at a corner table, until he called out: "Well hello Samantha – and you are looking wonderful too!" He gave her a hug and a kiss as she quickly apologised and admired his blue velvet smoking jacket, realising with relief that she had probably chosen the right outfit for the occasion.

"This is an amazing place," she told him as he helped her to take her place at the table. He pointed out that it was one of the special tables for *gaijin*, the Japanese name for foreigners, with a cut-out area to accommodate the diner's feet beneath the table to avoid squatting uncomfortably cross-legged throughout a long evening.

"I thought we should do something special," said Tom, and as they relaxed, one of the smiling geishas bowed and silently filled their sake cups for starters. "You deserve it, after all that you have been through," he added, raising his cup in a toast. "And I hope you are as happy as you look."

"Yes, I really am," she replied. "And it was not until we spent those few hours together in London a few weeks ago that I fully realised how important you have been for me. So thank you for inviting me here this evening and for everything you have done for me."

"Well, let's not dwell on the past now," he replied. "The future is more important and I want to tell you first why I am here in Tokyo. Actually, I am making a tour of all our overseas units to let everyone know that I am taking early retirement at the end of the year and that there will be an announcement soon about some organisational changes."

"Well, that's a big surprise, Tom," said Samantha, trying not to be distracted by two geishas who were laying out a wonderfully attractive spread of seafood delicacies on the table between them. "Is that what you really want? I would think you are too young to retire."

"Well, I am approaching my mid-fifties now," he answered. "And the civil service have an excellent retirement scheme for senior people. But more importantly, I have had a very demanding and stressful twenty years in MI5 as well as a couple of good promotions – but I am not likely to make the next step to Director. There are a couple of excellent younger candidates vying for that job when it comes up in a year's time".

"So what will you do? I still think you are too young to retire completely," she ventured.

"Well, lots of ideas but no plans as yet," he replied. "My brother and I inherited a lovely house in Scotland a couple of years ago. He is married but with no family and I am still on my own because my work has come first for too many years. Anyway, one idea is to turn the house into a small hotel and maybe run it jointly. Then I also have a couple of good friends in an international security company which is interested in using my experience in some way, but I am not sure I want that. I also want to find time to do some writing, so one way and another, I am not going to be idle."

As he was outlining his ideas, they also started to slowly enjoy each stage of the feast which seemed to keep coming, together with little ceremonies as the geishas identified and served the various dishes. They also regularly topped up the sake – and they had some fun together with the tradition of filling the cups to create a meniscus and then competing to see who could take a drink without spilling the tipple.

"I am sure you will not enjoy being idle," said Samantha, eventually returning to the subject of the future. "But whatever you decide and wherever you go, please let me stay in touch. As I said just now, since our meeting in London on my way to Japan I have realised just how special our relationship is. After all, you actually created Samantha Lord and gave me a new life and a new career when I was left for dead. There is nothing more special than that."

Tom took her hand across the table and getting a warm response, he moved around the table and sat beside her and put an arm around her. "The same goes for me too", he said with a gentle kiss on her cheek. "And when you tell me you have had enough of working for the CIA, I want to go on being part of your life as well."

"Then that could be very soon, Tom," she replied. "I have truly enjoyed being in the States and working with Bob and his team – a lot of wonderful experiences I never thought I would have. But I always knew that you would be there for me if I needed you. I don't want to let anybody down but if I could find a way to move on, I would do it. The problem is I do not know how?"

"When you are ready, that should not be a problem," Tom said, reassuringly. "The new identity team you worked with in the States can always do it again… and we have a group in the UK which has the same expertise". And with a quiet laugh, he added: "But don't change your hair style – I like you as a blonde."

She put her head on his shoulder and asked if the job of the identity team would include changing her name yet again. "I have never really felt like Samantha Lord," she added.

"Then I have a much better idea," said Tom, turning to look into her eyes. "How about becoming Marina again – or even Mrs. Marina Spencer?"

For a few moments, she could hardly believe what he had said. Then trying to compose herself, she asked: "What did you just say? Was that a proposal?"

Tom reached into his pocket and took out a small, blue velvet-covered box which he opened to show her a glistening gold ring with three sparkling diamonds and replied: "I cannot think of any better way to plan for my retirement than to share it with you, Marina. Since that first time I met you in the hospital in Germany I have known that you were the one girl in the world for me and over the many months since, I have come to love you very much, even from a distance."

Marina was thrilled, not least to hear him use her real name at last. She fought back her tears to slip the ring on to her finger and tell him: "Tom, I love you too, but I never imagined that you felt the same."

And as if by magic, the ever-observant geisha arrived at their table with two cut glass flutes and a bottle of Dom Perignon which she opened skilfully and gracefully filled the flutes before silently slipping away again.

"To us and a wonderful future," said Tom Spencer, as they raised their glasses.

Epilogue

During the following year, Tom Spencer's retirement from the British security services was the usual low key occasion – and so was his wedding a few weeks later. The couple retired to the house in the Scottish Highlands and it was hardly noticed when Tom's name appeared later in the Queen's Birthday Honours Civil Service list with a KCBE for "distinguished services".

So for Tom and Marina, it was new names again. They were now Sir Thomas and Lady Spencer and they settled quietly into a new life among their new neighbours, working mainly for local charitable organisations. And with time to reflect on their extraordinary experiences in the ruthless world of international espionage, they decided to try writing a spy novel... with a pen-name!

ABOUT THE AUTHOR

Peter Marshall's background includes service with the Royal Navy, and then journalism with the BBC, before moving to Visnews, the international TV news agency (now Reuters TV) where he became General Manager. This drew him into the satellite communications business, first in the UK and then in the USA for 14 years. In the UK he served as Chairman of the Royal Television Society, and in the USA he was elected to the Satellite Hall of Fame for his pioneering work in the use of communications satellites for the global transmission of TV news.

On his retirement, back in his native West of England, he began writing again and has worked as author or editor on a dozen books - on space flight, on travel and then two biographies. His first novel – *'The Russian Lieutenant'* - was partly inspired by his proximity to the tragic Novichok poisoning events in Salisbury and drew critical acclaim in both the UK and the USA. This described how an English career woman was drawn into a web of international intrigue through a dating website and the story continued in a second spy novel, *"Beyond the Funeral"*. The theme is now continued in this third spy novel.

Peter has drawn freely on his many years of global business travels and experiences to provide the framework for his ventures into the realms of fiction… and he is already planning a new spy story!

Other non-fiction books written and/or edited by Peter Marshall include:

The Oracle of Colombo
The World is Their Stage
Launching into Commercial Space
License to Orbit
Space Exploration and Astronaut Safety
MEGACRUNCH!

Lightning Source UK Ltd.
Milton Keynes UK
UKHW041435070122
396778UK00001B/42